Stephen

D1712843

Gary D Zackery & John Borgstedt

author**HOUSE**®

AuthorHouse™
1663 Liberty Drive
Bloomington, IN 47403
www.authorhouse.com
Phone: 1-800-839-8640

First published by AuthorHouse 1/20/2011

ISBN: 978-1-4567-2710-9 (e)
ISBN: 978-1-4567-2712-3 (dj)
ISBN: 978-1-4567-2711-6 (sc)

Library of Congress Control Number: 2011900295

Printed in the United States of America

Acknowledgements

As this work began, it was simply a short story for a young man that was experiencing the same difficulties all growing boys do. I had hoped to be able to present it to him as a means of helping him through those trying times. Unfortunately, circumstances did not allow that to happen and we were separated. There really is a Stephen out there and by now he is a fine young adult. His mother, Judy, was a very good friend and inspiration to me in many ways during the early period of this work. As a mother, she was also a fine inspiration to her son and daughter. I'd like to thank her for the brief time that we had together and the effect she had on my life and on this story.

My dear friend, Bob, was a primary source of agitation and prodding for me during the course of this work. His unfailing ability to draw out an idea and to always find that extra measure of color needed to flare the imagination to new heights is evident throughout the pages you are about to read. Without his constant oversight and nagging, this work would never have evolved into what it ultimately became. In light of all his literary abilities, his friendship has always been far more important still.

The art work for this book is by another good friend. I fell in love with Nick's work years ago and many of his paintings grace the walls of my home today.

Last but not least, I'd like to thank my wife, Diann, for all her labor and patience with me during the typing and retyping of the many rough drafts the manuscript went through. Her unfailing commitment to see it to its fruition was unparalleled. She is the picture of the perfect helpmate. You are my best friend, Diann. I love you!

Table of Contents

Author's Note

There are many tales of lands and peoples forgotten but for Legend. Each legend carries with it either a blessing or a curse and thereby gives purpose for its existence. This story is no different. I will leave it to your judgment as to its nature. I will only set the stage.

In a time long ago and in a land more rugged and violent, though simpler than our own, destinies and lives were being forged. It is to this land that one was born whom men called Stephen. Stephen was different from others around him, in that he refused to fear, and it was not in him to surrender to defeat. Not that his were a weak people; better to say they were simply worn down.

Stephen was a warrior, but he was more. And he was not a warrior, as most would recognize a man to be. Stephen did not glory in death or battle. He gloried in life and this was the motivation for his fighting; therefore, more were his inward battles than were his outward.

For those of you who deign to dine at the banqueting table on a tasty meal, the stage is set and you are offered a king's portion. Enjoy!

Wilderness of Cann

Preface

Dawn brought the promise of a beautiful day as the birds replaced the night noises with their voices of praise in agreement with the first streaks of color washing the Wilderness of Cann.

There was a rugged handsomeness in the mountain glades and valleys, and in the lands that spread distant as the winds. The lands stretched for miles, and few men there were who would not rightly call it a wilderness, yet it was not barren. There was a popular belief that it was called a wilderness, not because of what it was, but because of what it was not. It had been told in the stories of old that there were those who had known more promising lands, hence the calling of this land a wilderness. Rugged it was, and rugged were those who populated it. This is their story, as it has been passed down by the telling through the ages by the descendants of those tribes.

The Wilderness of Cann had a long history of turmoil and trouble. The land was inhabited by wandering tribes who tried endlessly to find a place of rest for their people, that is with the exception of the Giant Horsemen. The Giant Horsemen freely roamed over the vast expanse of the wilderness, bringing destruction and pain wherever their path led them. There was nothing holy to the Horsemen. They were a huge race, known for their cruelty and complete lack of conscience. Their chief weapons were fear, intimidation and their loud clamoring cries in the heat of battle. They traveled in packs and always sought out weak and helpless prey.

The Heart of the People

In the deep woods, there dwelt a small band of nomads known as the Peacemakers. They were a quiet people who trusted in the goodness of the Father of Spirits and lived from the fruit of the ground. Because they lived in such close communion with the land, the Peacemakers were a humble people, holding gentleness in high esteem.

They were a people made up of many tribes of the old country that had been brought together by the Great Hand of Mercy. In the early days, there were many peoples scattered over the old lands of Ability. Ability lay east of the Triall and was an ever-present reminder to the Peacemakers of the land they were now exiled from.

The river was, for the most part, feared by many who wandered in the wilderness; for, it was the great river that had separated them from their homeland. The river was believed to be the curse that kept them estranged from their heritage, thereby keeping them besieged by the evil ways of the Horsemen. Yet, it was this same river which forced them to seek every means possible to live peaceably together. Hence, their namesake.

According to the tales of the old men, there had been a change in the weather while the ancient tribes flourished in the homelands of Ability. The wisest among them held to the tale, which said that the lands only responded to the increasing coldness and barrenness in the hearts of the people.

Several destructive weather systems had blown through the land bearing winds and hail that left the expected harvest destroyed. The fields did not yield a crop the following harvest season, and the elders were sure there would be nothing but starvation should the people remain for the next planting. If they laid the last of their precious seed in barren ground, they would be hopeless if it yielded nothing. Their only hope was to find fertile ground. The land of Ability had been so decimated that it was decided there was no option for the tribes, but to gather together what could be carried and challenge the ravages of the Triall. It was told the tribes by some wanderer that the land across the great river was fertile and the water clear and good for drinking. It was to their misfortune that nothing had been told of the inhabitants of the southern and western region of the Wilderness of Cann. Yet, they gathered, by families, by tribes; huddled with their few possessions, all the tribes of Ability, not knowing where they would go, only believing that there was no longer a future for them in Ability.

Now, this was simply one of the more popular tales of their exodus. There were many others, some more interesting than the rest. One aspect of the true story was always left untold. Out of fear of the truth it held, or out of a dread for what it meant, it was never discussed and only the oldest of the tribesmen retained a spark of its existence.

The truth was that all did not leave Ability. The foolish wanderer who had brought false hope to the tribes of crossing the Triall had been spreading his delusions wherever he could find people without hope. But he did not find welcome with all. There were a few small groups in the land of Ability who had continued to believe that their Creator had not left them destitute. Though the land had not favored them with her fruit, their faith had remained in the Source of their provision. These brave hearts refused to leave the land they knew as home. For their faithfulness, they were all but forgotten by those who followed the wanderer.

True enough, the heart of most of the people had grown cold and as the land took on the nature of its inhabitants, the people then became bitter. Out of this condition came the desire to forsake the homeland. Most had come to regret the decision far sooner than the memory of their homeland faded. It seemed it was always there to remind them from where they had come, and it was made worse with every new discovery of the new land before them. A great foreboding soon set in when they beheld the signs of destruction that met them in Cann. It was then that they realized they had not entered a friendly country. This was a land of the survival of the fittest.

It was not clear how the tribes had come across the Triall. Many versions were often heard, but no one actually admitted to believing the tale that survived. It was said that after the gathering which followed the storm, the people had agreed to journey north in hope of finding better lands. As the people traveled, they came within sight of the lands of Faate. The blood of the people turned cold in their veins. The Triall was said to then have frozen over and the tribes, in a panic, rushed across the great river. The people, seeing what their departure from the old ways had brought them, sat down and wept. As they wept, the tears drained down to the river and melted the Triall, this sealing the people in the Wilderness of Cann.

The Triall River came down from the icy lands of Faate. No one inhabited the land of Faate. In fact, there was not so much as a rumor of anyone successfully attempting to travel into the land. A few tales of failure had survived longer than their subjects. It was said that even animals would not go there. The water of the Triall near Faate was so cold it was usually afloat with great pieces of ice. Even the fish rarely traveled upstream to the high places of the great river.

On the western side of the river the assembled multitude, who now called themselves the Peacemakers, were forced to travel down stream away from the frozen land of Faate, deep into the Wilderness of Cann.

The southern and western borders of the wilderness were bound by the Vale of Nott. By all accounts, the Horsemen had originated from deep within the Vale. The Vale was a foreboding land, full of harsh mountains, bleak volcanic fields and the stench of sulfur.

While tales of people successfully journeying to Faate did not exist, there were many tales of those who journeyed to Nott and returned. However, they always seemed to return forever changed by whatever it was they experienced. The one thing that they all held in common was their silence about what they had seen. And there remained a hardness, even a downright meanness in them. Few cared to journey to Nott after seeing the hollowness of those who returned.

Thus was the lay of the lands and its inhabitants, for it was a simple world. But things awaited that would turn this simple world into a battlefield of conflict and turbulence.

A Child Is Formed

A people are measured by the scope of their dreams, and there remained an ever present hope in the heart of every member of the clan that there would be one to come who would bring them deliverance, and maybe even find the means to return them to their homeland. Though their vision of the homeland existed only in story and song, the people held the hope for a better way of life, as the old legends passionately proclaimed.

The constant harassment from the Horsemen and the traumatic strain that was ever present in the clan because of the recurrent raids yielded a low birth rate among the Peacemakers. Some that did come to birth were stillborn and even more were lame.

The clan became excited at the prospect of any birth. There was speculation and the general atmosphere of the village would become very charged, in hope of a healthy child.

The average person of the tribe was of medium to small stature, brown to black hair and dark eyes. Yet there was a child born under a full moon in the season of the coming forth of flowers that brought not a small stir in the village. Especially so, as the midwife made it her duty to go about the village whispering of the birth of a beautiful, large, fair-headed and blue eyed male child born in the dwelling of Dunn and Aieda.

If the tribe was not already delighted with the latest marvel, they were to be pressed even further with the giving of the child's name. Dunn stood before the assembled gathering and cradled his son in his arms. As a semblance of quiet was established, he said, "He shall be called Stephen after his great-great grandfather, born under the same moon and with the same features. As he was a mighty man of our people, so this child shall also be!"

This did nothing to end the murmurs, in fact it only lent fuel to the fire. Now there had also been a foretelling!

Life became more complicated upon this addition to their dwelling and the new parents began to appreciate their own love for one another as they recognized the need for it in their newborn son. He was not a difficult child, but he had his own way and required a greater amount of consideration.

Aieda was the first to voice her appraisal of this, along with her consternation. "I have never seen a child who required so much from a parent, yet he does not allow me to protect him or to be too close to him for long. It is as though he wants for me to provide him that which he cannot get on his own, then he wants to be left to his own inventions. It surely perplexed me in the beginning, but I have come to respect this in him and allow him to grow and develop in accordance with his needs."

Dunn sat listening and for a long moment after she finished, watched Stephen in the corner of the dwelling. He was placing small clay figures in columns, then reordering them in circles, as though trying to make up his mind which would be the most advantageous were he in war or in counsel.

"Yes, I too have noticed what you speak of. I do not say that I was at all comfortable with his behavior at the beginning, but I have come to understand. It appears the child possesses such awareness even in these early years; he is far more advanced even than ourselves, that his actions and habits are uncommon to us. Yet, they are most natural to him. We have nothing to be alarmed about, as you have affirmed. We must only appreciate him and help him in whatever small ways we are appointed by the Father of Spirits."

As the child matured, his parents became convinced that their estimation of his future was correct. As testament to this, the child's rearing became of interest to the elders of the clan.

Dunn sat beside a stream mending baskets used for trapping fish as a voice spoke from behind him. "Have you the need of another hand, Dunn?"

Turning to look upon his visitor, he was pleased to see the familiar wrinkled and toughened face, yet still alive with the fire and joy of love, of the man he looked to both as a father and friend. Jared was the father of Teldig, a man as close to Dunn as his own brother. Jared had been chosen to speak to Dunn of the elders' request.

"Well, if a man was of a mind to get his feet wet, and would not object to sharing in the profit of so doing, then I suppose you could say that a hand would be welcomed of that man. But, if you suggest that I would be inclined to accept the labor of a man who did not consider himself worthy of his wage, then you would be mistaken."

Jared's hearty laughter broke the long silence as he pondered Dunn's reply and Dunn stood as they embraced one another. Dunn waved to the baskets nearby that he had finished mending. Each of them picked one up and the two men eased their way into the water to secure them to the bottom of the stream in the slow moving water.

In a few minutes, having finished their task, they moved back up and onto the bank. Dunn moved back onto his rock he had been sitting on while he repaired the baskets and motioned for Jared to do the same. "What could be so important to bring a busy man as yourself to wade around in the cold waters of Cann with a loner such as the one before you?"

Jared feigned innocence and hurt then broke into a gentle smile. "First of all, your company would be enough to bring any reasonable man to such a low state! Was I not at your table a few days ago? And did I not ask you to accompany me to rebuild the perimeter posts not more than two moons ago?"

Jared hunched his shoulders as if impatient for a reply, then rushed on so that none could be made. "But you are right. There is something that has come up. Dunn nodded his head. "See, I knew it!"

"Am I to be condemned before I make my argument?"

"No, no. Go ahead. I just thought it may be important for me to see where we stood from the beginning."

The jesting having run its course, Jared waved the air as if to push the conversation away and went on, "The elders have come to believe that Stephen may well be the one who has been spoken of in the old stories. I have been chosen to present you with the idea of the child being fostered by the elders. Mind you, it would not be a total separation from your dwelling, but he would spend a great deal of time with the elders being trained in the tribal customs, traditions of the Peacemakers and the ideas of leadership."

Jared noticed Dunn's downcast eyes and wondered if he had not committed a grievous act against his friend. Dunn's silence affirmed all that his look suggested. When he finally spoke, his tone was low and his words came slowly.

"Aieda, I ah... Look, Jared, Stephen is ... yes he is different. And he may very well be, as you say, the one foretold. You know that I do not mean this as an accusation against you personally, but you know that Aieda and I do not agree with many of the things that are done and said by the elders of the clan. For the most part, they are nothing more than self appointed men who desire prominence and respect without having to come by it honestly."

He tried to calm himself and be honest about his thoughts without hurting Jared. "We suspected that something of this nature would happen sooner or later, if what we thought concerning Stephen was true, since we have seen that our child is more honorable in his ways than those who now propose to teach him. And having already sought the Father of Spirits' desire in this, Aieda and I feel that Stephen's best training will come from his own dwelling. We do not wish to be seen as overprotective parents nor as rebellious clan members, but we are certain about this and will not be moved."

Dunn's thoughts returned once again to his own parents, now long since called home by another of the Horsemen's merciless raids. He remembered again his father, Dursis' words to him, "Your mother and I have always sought to train you up in the nurture and instruction of the Sure Hand, with the knowledge that when our work is complete and you are your own man, we will not be ashamed to know you as our son and you will remain on the path of love and obedience."

Their method had not failed and Dunn was grateful to have had the benefit of their love, counsel and discipline. He was one of the most respected, if not the most appreciated, clansman of the tribe. Yet, he had never once even considered it to be so.

Silence enveloped the two of them again and they sat as two men who had said goodbye to a long time adversary, then Jared spoke, "I am relieved, Dunn. The truth is that I did not desire this. I had even seen it coming and tried to dissuade several of the elders ahead of time, but they would not be swayed. They were determined to have him and demanded my cooperation. I know I could have dissented and relinquished my position to the fool-headed, but would not the clan be the worse off for it, with one less voice who at least desires their good?"

He let his question hang in the air a moment, stood and embraced his friend again and said, "I am sorry I had to be the one to ask, but I am glad it was no other. Know that I am with you and the child is in the very best of care possible in the dwelling of Dunn and Aieda. His peace remain in your midst."

Jared did not await Dunn's reply, but turned and left immediately. Dunn sat back down on his rock and thought for a long time about all that had transpired and the more that was to come.

With these events in mind, he returned home with renewed vigor and a deeper commitment and desire to give his son all that he could to be the man that he was surely born to be. The dreams that were already being revealed in Stephen became a constant reminder of their task and responsibility to prepare and uphold him as he reached for those goals. With this in mind, his parents instilled both love and discipline in double portion in Stephen.

As he grew, life took on a very serious nature with Stephen. His family, his people and his unseen homeland were as one burden in his heart and he carried them with him always, as he did the pain he felt for them. Knowing that his people had no home, no permanent place of rest, he cherished a dream that they would one day break lose from the controlling terror that the Horsemen had brought upon them. He could not bring himself to accept the idea of being a slave to the evil desires of another. He would willingly die a thousand deaths himself for his people to be able to stand straight and tall once more. Somehow, he knew man was not meant to live in bondage to a man or the fear of a man. Life was to be lived in freedom and joy...the same joy that Stephen had deep within himself, yet a joy never understood or experienced by the others of his clan. His people were just not open to this type of behavior, not as far back he could remember, anyway.

It would have sounded foolish beyond measure to try to explain his experiences to anyone. Although his closest companions had glimpses of it, they still were far from understanding that Stephen had, beyond even his comprehension, come to the realization that one day he would be the leader of his people, and that he would be that one to lead them back to the homeland.

Stephen wore his inner knowledge as a quiet burden. It wasn't awkward to him, but rather, it gave even his joy a studied seriousness. When called to greatness, the heart within cannot help but affirm its call while acknowledging the vast forces at work which are out of its control to accomplish. If Stephen but knew... these were the things kings were made of! So, he lived. And he waited for the appointed time, which he knew not.

Stephen was twelve full cycles in the time of flowers. He was already the best hunter; he could run faster, shoot with the long bow further and wrestle better than any his age. He had already become the envy of most within a few cycles about him.

The children of the Peacemakers were taught early that the development of their physical skills were to be balanced by and always secondary to their spiritual and mental development. In this, Stephen excelled all.

Twelve cycles was considered to be the active age among the Peacemaker; the age of responsibility. It was at this age that the young began to intermingle. Before the twelfth cycle, male and female children were kept separate, for the most part. Not because of law, but simply because the boys were found with their father working the field, building pens for the animals, mending broken fences, training with the other boys or in the woods hunting game. Daughters were mainly found with the women of the clan learning to prepare dwellings, cook and preserve foods, tan skins and make suitable, functional clothing.

A ceremony known as First Hunt was observed by the clan for the boys coming to their twelfth cycle. The young men were sent out for the duration of the growing season. Each First Hunt held its own feeling of excitement for the boys, namely because no one ever went on a twelfth cycle hunt more than once. The purpose of the hunt was to give the young men an opportunity to learn to depend upon one another for their survival and for each one to find his own tribal position. Every hunt after the First Hunt was strictly for survival.

Every boy sought the Father of Spirits for special favor during the hunt, recognizing the need for wisdom and might greater than his own. Many times there was occasion to give thanks for such seeking. It was not unusual for the young men to return with unimaginable tales of cunning and acts of strength that were displayed by their fellow hunters. The tales were very helpful in raising the anticipation of the younger boys of the village, who would soon be going on their own First Hunt. The Peacemakers enjoyed, above all else, watching their young draw near to the Creator in physical maturity, mental development and the blossoming of the spiritual world in their eyes. It was this knowledge of their Creator, which bought the great peace for which they were named.

In the twelfth cycle, the older women of the clan would take the young women aside and begin an intensive time of training in healing medicines, herbs, and plants; for their knowledge would soon be needed to mend sore and aching bodies, and the wounded of battle. Equally important were the teachings of the powerful strengths exhibited in supporting, caring for and loving a mate in all forms. These secrets were added to the young woman's wealth of knowledge already gained from her mother and the other women of the clan.

By the end of the twelfth cycle, a young woman would be ready for the time of promise, which usually began with the return of the young men of the First Hunt, and ending a few cycles later with the pledging ceremony. Only then could she explore her treasure chest of knowledge and loving which had been deposited within her during the twelfth cycle.

While the hunters were away, the young women would prepare the village for their much-anticipated return. There would be much meat to preserve and much celebration. They considered it a privilege to welcome the hunters home, for the boys who left would be returning as young men!

Much was learned from those months spent in the wilderness. Families would observe quietly, watching for the ties of permanent bonding to be formed...marriages yet to be promised would be speculated upon, friendship bonds which would serve for strong neighbors or war allies were knitted. No one pushed the young adults into relationships, for it was a matter of the heart in all bonding.

Stephen knew that his twelfth cycle hunt would be even more special than usually expected. He had come to understand that the vision he had would soon blossom in the hearts of his clansmen. It was his highest desire for them to begin to glimpse that dream. To his brave heart's delight, this was to be his hunt, and he knew it with every fiber of his being.

Sunrising of the Heart

"What was your first hunt like, Father? I know it was exciting. What I mean is, was it anything different from other first hunts; and were there any significant things that were worthy of being retold and recalled?" Stephen's voice was low and his demeanor suggested that he had been contemplating these things for some time. He waited calmly for his father to answer.

"I was not the aggressive hunter when I was young, as most boys strive to be. I did not participate in the youthful games with as much fervor as my companions and therefore did not excel in those areas. Much time was spent with my father and Jared, who was his closest clan-brother. They were all my world needed! In those days, I could not envision a world without Jared and my father as the center of all that happened with me.

"The hunt was pleasantly remembered. But what stands out in memory now, after all these years, is that I saw then those who would become the future foundation stones of this tribe. I saw as well those who would become the stumbling blocks; both have remained faithful to their course."

"What did it teach you? I feel there is something I am to learn from this hunt. I also believe that it will be anything but uneventful."

"I am sure that when your time comes, you will rise to the task and all that you have gained to this day will be at your disposal.

"To answer your question, I believe that I learned that whatever a man is made of, that is the essence of all he will ever become. Yet, it remains for some men to be nurtured and led. The deep water of their souls may only come forth through enduring love and much patience, and this, my son, will prove to be your greatest test."

His mind filled with new thoughts, Stephen found his covering and drifted off to another world of dreams and kingdoms yet to be established.

In the early morning light, the air was chilled in the dwelling. Stephen stretched, quickly threw off the covering skins and crouched near the small fire where Aieda, his mother, was preparing the herb broth and the first meal of the day. He saw a stack of fresh traveling-food cakes, still warm and flooding the area with their aroma. He was tempted to reach for one, but an admonishing glance from Sister Keene held him fast. He would soon have his fill, but it would not be within the protection of the shelter with its closeness and love.

Stephen had slept remarkably well. Not so with many of the others who were also rising to their day of The First Hunt. Many had tossed the night away with anxiety and uncertainty. Stephen's sound sleep was brought about in part by the understanding of a loving family who had prepared their firstborn son well, not to mention the fact that Dunn had held him to an exceptionally strenuous day of hard work! Stephen questioned him about the seemingly excessive amount of labor, as they stacked another pile of wood, in the springtime!

"May I ask why we are cutting and stacking wood in the spring? And why have we run your fish baskets four times today? And why, may I ask, did you see fit to wake me this morning before daylight?"

"Why Stephen, I felt that we might share the burdens of the dwelling while there were many hands present for the labor!"

Stephen's consternation brought a brief chuckle from his father. They finished their last stack of wood and went inside the dwelling for a delicious and well deserved meal followed by a story, as was their custom, and a good night's rest.

Because of his father's dedication to discipline and integrity, Stephen came by his wisdom honestly. And because he recognized these signs in his father, obedience was not a burden to him. He found it a delight to please him simply by obeying him.

Stephen sat securely surrounded by his close knit family, his heart filled with wonder, sipping the thick, rich broth made by his mother, Aieda efficiently fed portions to everyone as she prepared the last of the traveling-cakes for Stephen's journey.

His mood was evident to his mother and she reached out to him. He saw her offered hand and took it into his own. She spoke softly to him as only a mother can. "You know that we have ever been here for you. In this time when you will not have the benefit of our fellowship, guidance and strength, you will realize afresh the presence of your truest Friend. He is ever with you and His love will keep you. Call upon Him and He will answer you. Know Him as your ever faithful Creator and you will want for nothing, even in the time of testing. He is All in all. Do not be afraid, Stephen. Do not be anxious for anything. All will be given as it is required."

He was amazed again with her ability to see inside of him. Those thoughts were there again, risen from that dark place where they hid, waiting for a chance to assail him. She had noticed his inner struggle as he considered all that lay before him. Would he fail? Would he lose the faith that had been such a driving force all his life? Worse yet, would the vision fail? How could it? And then, what was to ensure that it could not? This last thought brought Stephen to a new understanding and to a new height. It was not the vision that contained any great significance. The vision itself was only the idea. And the idea possessed no power of its own.

A fresh picture burst into his sight. He saw a tool, a lever. The lever lay lifeless. He also saw the concept of the lever; man channeling multiple times his own strength through the working out of an idea. Then Stephen understood why failure was not an issue any longer. He realized that he was the tool, the vision was the idea and the Giver of the Vision was the power that moved the lever. Doubt gave way to faith and as he lifted his eyes over the hills before their dwelling, sunlight spilled over into the valley of the Peacemakers.

Saying goodbye was difficult, but was eased by the fervent expectations of a joyous return, and the entrusting of one another's hearts to the Sprit of Goodness. And so, the time came for the joining up of the child-men hunters and for their departure.

As Dunn stood alongside his son, he reached into his leather sheath and slipped something cold and keen into Stephen's hand. Without looking down, Stephen's heart began racing and a bead of sweat traced his brow. He knew immediately what had just happened and the significance of it brought to him sensations he had never experienced. Dunn had never been seen without this knife. Stephen knew its history by heart. Generations of his forefathers had passed this same knife from father to son as their token of supreme trust and the distinguishing mark of the family custodian.

Tears formed in his eyes as he opened his hand to behold the sign of his family's confidence. Father of Spirits be praised! It was good to walk among such people!

With mixed feelings, the entire village gathered to send off her sons. Fare-thee-wells were said all around. Not a few mothers' tears were shed, for mothers were a tender creation. None were without the knowledge that First Hunts were often last Hunts for many. Yet, what life would be worth living were it forever sheltered? Its fullness among the Peacemakers was measured not in quantity of years, but rather in degree of fulfillment. Tales abounded among the Peacemakers of both young and old men of renown...and yes, women as well.

As the boys made preparations to be off, all those left in the village were extremely excited for them. However, the boys themselves were somewhat withdrawn. They were uncertain just exactly how they would fare over the next few months, all except Stephen, that is. Stephen was filled with such zeal he could hardly contain himself! This was what he had waited so long for! The dream was finally taking on some real meaning. Surely, it would not be long before the whole village would begin to see. And it would start right in the midst of these young hunters! After so long a time of wandering around in the wilderness, he would see now the Father of Spirits get the attention of His people.

Stephen made effort to concentrate on the hunt, for he was being taken up again with his imaginings and longings for that Higher Life.

Although Stephen was unaware of it, those he had grown up among were quite accustomed to his "daydreaming." Most simply shrugged it off as a passing thing of youth. While he did not live his life in such a way as to please the minds of others, he was ever mindful of maintaining their respect and setting an example for those who would follow in his steps.

Little did Stephen know that the Father of All had instilled the seed of these same dreams in all His creation. Many denied it, many failed to believe it, and more still feared it. Yet, there remained the seed of this dream within a few who cherished it even though they could not possibly begin to understand it. Each thought it foolish and impossible, while fiercely refusing to surrender it.

The Giant Horsemen

The sanctity of the village was burst upon by the screaming cry of ten Horsemen as they raced through the middle of the village. People scattered in every direction. A rope was dragged behind each horse with a hook shaped object attached to it. As a horseman rode by a dwelling, a sharp turn of his horse would bring the dwelling crashing down behind him.

The Horsemen wore their jet black hair in long full braids with bone fragments woven throughout. Their faces were covered with horrible leather masks, said to be the skin removed from the faces of their many victims. Where the hoof prints of the Horsemen remained, the smell of death usually permeated the air as well for days.

The horses were arrayed in the same manner as their riders. They were battle trained to bite, and to maul and destroy with their fierce hooves.

Riding these awesome beasts, swinging their huge war clubs and carrying lances the thickness of a man's arm; the Giant Horsemen were a terrible sight.

They seemed to have vanished as quickly as they appeared, although the evidence of their raid was plainly visible. At least six dwellings were completely demolished and several were badly damaged. Crying children filled the village adding to the confusion.

When most of the children had been comforted and everyone was sure that there was no loss of life, the elders assembled in the Place of Gathering. The men of the village had erected a large pavilion type covering that served for clan gatherings, harvest time work and many other like functions. It was located in the center of the village.

The injuries were minimal, as well as could be determined. The exception being the spirits of the women who had lost their dwellings. The dwelling places were esteemed by the women who built them as highly as a father would esteem his son. Not because of the material value, but because the clan believed that it's whole foundation was based in the dwelling, everything began there. A man received his strength from having a good, healthy atmosphere in his dwelling, and that was a direct result of his wife's ability to make it so. Likewise, well balanced, healthy children came from healthy and safe dwellings.

The first question would normally have been how to go about aiding those women whose dwellings would require attention or even rebuilding, at any other time that is. But this was not a normal time. This was the day of First Hunt. Nothing short of disaster stopped the Hunt. So, now it was left to the elders to drive away the remaining fear and confusion in the village and get the hunters off. The sooner they left, the sooner other matters could be looked to. This would take some considerable ingenuity, seeing that most of the village was more or less in a state of disarray. The sending forth of the hunters was to be a joyous affair, but how was anyone to be joyous in the wake of this recent raid.

Stephen made his way down the path to the Place of Gathering chanting a song from his childhood. The song was known by all in the clan, yet was not often heard. The reason was that the song intimidated most. However, Stephen made the song bend to his stature. Those hearing it noticed that it sounded fresh, as if it were being sung now for the first time. It was wonderful. Neither the quality nor the richness of the voice held such attraction, but the pouring forth of one's soul in purity and innocence was captivating.

No one thought to wonder why anyone would be singing at a time like this. It was the furthest thing from each mind. The only thought that arose was that this was what men were made for, this song, and this boy singing this song. He was painting a scenery in their spirits of life, peace and serenity. They wished the song to never end. They hungered for the feeling to go on forever.

By the time Stephen reached the Place of Gathering, a following had grown behind him. As he came to stand before the elders, the song faded away and he recognized by the silence in the village that the entire clan had stopped what they were doing and were listening to his song. He was quite amazed by their reaction, as he had only come here to see if maybe he could be of any help to the elders. He was only singing to himself because it helped him focus his attention away from himself. He was wondering again why these people so often behaved so strangely.

It suddenly occurred to each of the elders that their dilemma had resolved itself without their intervention. They stood speechless looking to one another for an explanation. The assembly dispersed, and Stephen was left standing before the Place of Gathering... wondering if he may have missed something.

The clan instinctively moved toward the village entrance. As the thought of the Horsemen and their terror was replaced by the peace and tranquillity of the song, so now was the latter replaced with the thrill of the Hunt.

Outward Bound

All the time spent dreaming of a bright future seemed to be finally paying off for Stephen; he was going on his First Hunt! After the shouts and exclamations of joy, the boys were saluted and sent off. It was close to noon before the boys were in a state of mind to consider why exactly they were walking into the middle of a wilderness.

Stephen had not joined in on the celebrating and jousting about. He had actually been more silent than usual. A few of the boys turned around to be sure he was still with the hunting party. His attention seemed strangely drawn to his surroundings. He didn't hear the great black bear story of a boy's forefather, or the many names of the girls that would be waiting on their return, nor was he aware of anything else in this physical realm. Stephen was listening with all his might to the voice that spoke ever so gently within him, leading him... no, wooing him into the wilderness.

The peaceful feeling of being carried along was the only thing he could sense, until late that afternoon. One of the boys pulled his arm and it took a moment before he could get Stephen's attention.

"Stephen! Do you see it?"

With that, he was brought back to the sight of a large mountain cat moving in the woods, far down the valley from where they were walking. Suddenly, the cat sprang forward with a noticeable gait and the heart of every boy experienced the same lurch. They were each looking at one another with the same questioning glance.

"What do we do, now?"

Not a word was spoken as they saw the cat edging closer. By this time they could see that the cat stood well over a bow's length tall and seemed to be at the least a full spear shaft long from head to tail! The fear began to mount in the boys by the second. They were certain of only one thing, there were not many seconds left, if something were to be done to lengthen their lives.

The heart of every boy froze as Stephen leaped from his stooped position and ran toward the cat.

"Just what is he doing? Is he crazy?"

Panic was in every word. None moved to strengthen Stephen's defense.

"He'll be eaten alive! That cat is nearly twice his size!"

It was evident to all that shock had taken its toll on the party; they were completely disarmed.

Stephen had now taken cover in the woods and could be seen only briefly as he maneuvered his way around the area where the cat had paused to survey its method of attack. The cat lifted its head to sniff the air, which blew Stephen's scent to it as a warning and turned to enter the woods. Stephen merged with the shadows and disappeared.

He knew that danger was eminent, yet fear did not register. He calculated his steps with a hunter's accuracy and put his whole focus on his prey. He had never once seen himself as prey, which proved to be his greatest weapon.

The smell of the wild caught his nostrils as he heard the light breathing of the cat and knew it was near. He had hoped to be the first to gain sight. He would now have to depend upon his ability to bring the battle without the element of surprise.

The big cat lunged for Stephen as he made his way around a huge maple. Massive claws ripped the leather clasps that held his breeches together. Dark red droplets sprinkled the ground beneath him. Stephen's instincts were on the ready and his hunting club found its mark as the feline posed to make another lunge; she went down.

Although she was wounded, dead she was not. Before Stephen had time to pull his father's knife, no....his knife, the cat had sprung to her feet and was about to gain her senses. Stephen gave another swing of his club and now wasted no time unsheathing the hunting knife. Before the cat's heart stopped beating, he had opened its throat with precision and swiftness.

Lying on the ground beside the maple, in the mingled blood of prey and hunter, was a huge broken tooth, the result of Stephen's first blow.

He cut a couple of strips from the bottom of his britches and fastened the torn portion together, picked up the cat's broken jaw tooth and made his way to the clearing where the other hunters had huddled after he had disappeared into the woods.

Stephen shared the details of the kill with is brothers and before he could finish they were all beside themselves with excitement. After his boisterous companions settled down a bit, he explained how the jaw tooth had fallen in his own blood beside the tree and that he felt a great import from this. He started to explain what he saw from it and was lost in the other boys rehearsals of the episode. He felt stunned as he recognized that what he was saying had no bearing on them; as though they didn't even hear him! This was more important than the kill, yet they could not hear it! It had taken the shedding of blood to bring their deliverance from this creature; and not without loss of life.

Stephen was filled with wonder and praise to the Great Overseer for His protection and deliverance, and that he had found such favor.

As the boys all pitched in to skin the cat, Stephen's blade worked quickly and efficiently. The clamor around him had brought new seriousness to him, and the boys murmured in confusion to see the tears in the eyes of their brother. He had just come to the realization that it had cost a life to make him great.

This new revelation caused fresh concern; the people would not understand. He wished only for them to recognize the love and goodness of the Father of Spirits. He knew how easy it was for them to focus on what they could see only with the natural eye. Rarely did he ever know of anyone catching even a glimpse of the dreams and visions that made up such a large degree of his life. He knew that the greatest obstacle to leading his people would be to instill in them the vision of where they were going. Without a vision, they were sure to perish.

That first day of the hunt brought the boys deeper into the wilderness than any of them had ever been before. The Triall River had been their guide for the latter part of the day, and by nightfall, the banks of the river were lowering and a sandy beach had unfolded itself to the young hunters. Deciding they had reached an agreeable place to bed down for the night, camp was made. After the excitement of their first day out, the evening had seemed to rob them of their strength. Quietly, one by one, sleep claimed them.

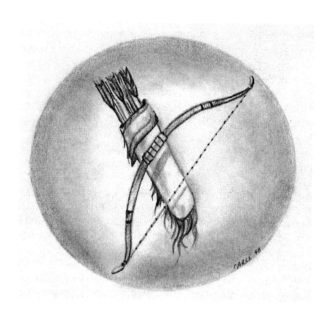

Every Hunter's Pack Full

As the new dawn broke over the horizon, a racket could be heard in the distance. The boys began to stir as their curiosity was piqued. They arose to discover Stephen putting together some type of table using fresh limbs that had been stripped of bark. Not understanding the purpose for this early morning exercise, rubbing sleep from their eyes, they inquired as to what he was up to. He simply nodded to his left and continued his work. There on the ground were a mess of fish and several handfuls of edible roots. He had been up long before dawn and had already gathered a morning meal for everyone. This fair-hair was one interesting brother indeed! Not one of the boys regretted having him in their midst. Not one would fail to follow him to the ends of the earth, if need be.

The boys spent their days running the length of the valleys and climbing endless hilltops. The freedom of the wilderness was enough to keep most of them captivated in thought the majority of the time, as they discovered first hand all that their elder clansmen had taught them concerning plants and animals…and life! The days passed more quickly than any of the boys would have desired.

As the time of harvest drew near, the hunters began to make their way back to their village. They had killed many small brown bear that were common to the wilderness, which were not extremely large, but were known for having a real mean streak. There were also many beaver, turkey, and deer. The boys had cached quite a collection of hides and dried meat, and had become excellent bowmen and trackers.

Things began to take on a more serious tone as the hunt neared its end. The hunters knew that their time was limited and what they accomplished would have long lasting effects. Their future tribal position was in the balance and there were many waiting back home to see how their young men had fared. They were not to be disappointed. None of these hunters were going to come home empty handed. As they neared home on the return trip, cache after cache added to the bounty which the young men gladly shouldered. By the time they reached the camping place for their last night out, they were bone weary, yet greatly pleased with their vast collection of pelts and meats.

Youthful bodies were tight, tanned and well muscled, hands were strong and callused, feet were toughened, shoulders broadened by the burdens and eyes clear with the knowledge of a life well lived. There was not one among them who could not manage to light a fire, dig roots, make a medicine poultice, brew an herb tea, plan a stealthy approach to game, sharpen a lance, fashion a carry basket or all of a hundred other tasks necessary to sustain life or help make it easier for a brother.

Stephen was amazed to see that there was always someone who had the ability to fill the need of the moment, as he also recognized that everyone did not excel at everything. This was good, in that every person was forced to humble himself and learn from or be helped by his brother. It had taken the whole season and then some, but these young men were a working team which anyone would have been proud to be a part of.

Tired as they were, they all enjoyed the fellowship and closeness of one last night around the campfire. Eventually, even the stout hearted were suppressing yawns. Reluctantly, each one yielded to the night with a heart full of the thoughts of battle and victory. None would be found lacking on either account.

Last Day Out

Dawn found Stephen on a hill overlooking the camp. He had been stirred in his spirit in the night and found himself lying half-awake when he decided he might as well be up, so he had walked until he came upon this bluff. As the cool wind from the approaching autumn blew across the hills of the Wilderness of Cann, Stephen stood gazing out over the treetops of the valley below.

He had grown a great deal in understanding over the last few months. He was very much looking forward to seeing his family and secretly he cherished the thought of standing alongside his father again, not as an equal, but just to see how he "measured up."

He had learned so much about his Creator from all that he had witnessed during his hunt. Like the way the small animals on the ground received their portion of food when the wind and rain beat the berries and other food stuffs from the trees. Or the way the old leaves and twigs provided material for the nests of the friends in the skies. And the way the ants were always the first to know of coming rain, and built up their mounds to protect from the risk of high water drowning their people. By watching the wisdom in these small creatures, man was able to prepare for the rains himself. Stephen was always looking to these events as signs of his own Creator's wisdom and love toward His creation.

Remembering the long journey ahead for the hunting party, Stephen turned back towards the camp where the others were packing the remainder of their gear. It would be a tiring day by its end, and he wanted to get started as soon as possible. Much rough country lay ahead and there were many hides and much meat to carry. The hunters had done well, thus far.

No one noticed as Stephen made his way over to his bedroll and began gathering up his gear. There was almost a melancholy atmosphere but he shrugged it off. It wasn't long before everyone was ready and they made off with hopeful hearts and a tinge of longing for home.

Stephen glanced at each of his friends as they trudged along and wondered at how they were relating to all that they had experienced. He wished somehow he could help them to see all that he had seen. But he knew that everything had its own time and season. Patience would have her perfect work. If the Father of Spirits could wait for the perfecting of His people, Stephen too could wait. But it was still hard at times to be patient about something which was so important to him.

The hunters were now spread out along a trail through a large area of woods that was covered with bear tracks, which seemed to indicate a family of three, maybe four big Black Bear. The anticipation was strong among the hunters and the blood was racing in their veins. The Black Bear they had seen this cycle had all been larger than usual, due to the excessive rains and migration of fish moving upstream on the Triall. There was so much food for the bears, they were nearly twice their normal size, and meaner than ever, too. So, the hunters were excited at the prospect of bagging a whole family, and bringing fresh bear meat to the village for a welcome feast!

A loud scream to the far right of the hunters turned every head like a whirlwind. There was not a doubt in the mind of any what that scream meant; one of them had been caught off guard by one of the big Blacks! Terror seized them at the thought of the pain that must have brought forth such a terrible sound.

When the hunters came upon the area of the attack, the ground was covered with the fresh red life of a young hunter the others knew as Cutter. His left arm was nearly severed and his back badly lacerated by the long razor claws of the huge Black. Cutter had dragged himself into the cleft of a cluster of trees whose branches were intertwined. The bear was trying frantically to get at his prey, but Cutter was just beyond his reach, though not as far out of reach as he would have preferred.

At the sight of the other hunters, the bear turned and let out a great roar. He was not in the least afraid of them, and it seemed he was intent to do damage to each one, if necessary.

While a few of them coaxed the Black away from the clump of trees and the wounded Cutter, a couple of the others were able to pull their fallen brother up onto a rocky cliff a good distance away. By now, the bear was kicking up dust at the boys and clawing at the air with incredible force. If he was trying to intimidate them, he was doing a terrific job! Most of them were moving....stumbling backwards over logs and anything else in the way. In their fear, they were acting as individuals again, and not as a team.

Stephen was watching them, as if searching for something that was hidden somewhere in their midst. Surely, he thought, one will take the initiative. But as he watched them all retreat, compassion began to rise up in his heart for them. He was seeing the very problem that had kept his people in bondage for so long. Fear had conquered their will to fight; to fight their real enemy of self-preservation and complacency.

The bear was about to corner a couple of the boys in a clump of woods too thick to back out of. Just then, the other two Blacks emerged from the riverbank, and it was plain that they were not of gentle spirit.

Stephen gathered all his strength and with a silent prayer, he raced towards the giant Black with a hatchet held high over his head. He sunk the head deep into the neck of the raging Black. As it turned to claw Stephen, its head drooped to one side, and as if a great wind had blown upon him, he fell with a great earth-shaking thud.

Stephen wasted no time turning to rush in the direction of the two approaching Blacks. As soon as he had their attention (one small easy meal was more inviting than a whole group) he ran back in the direction of the woods that the hunting party had just exited, so he would be on familiar ground. As he ran, he picked up small stones, throwing them at the bears to keep their mind on their meal. He would run ahead a bit and then throw another couple of rocks. As soon as he had them a good distance from the other hunters, he notched an arrow and with concentrated effort, he gently released the string. He wasted no time sending forth a second and neither missed its mark. A great shrieking gasp escaped the breast of the mama Black as she stumbled forward.

Stephen turned to run again. The yearling, which could hardly be called a cub for its size, had not even broke pace as his mother had fallen to the ground. Stephen once more stopped, turned and reached for yet another arrow, only to realize that his quiver was empty. His arrows must have dislodged while he ran.

"Now what?" His thoughts raced over the terrain that was a road map in his mind, and a plan began to form.

Remembering a stone ledge not far back up the trail, he ran with all his might in hope that he had the energy to get there in one piece, and that his desire to do so was greater than this Black's appetite and anger.

The bear continued its bundling gallop and was getting well lathered in the process. By the time Stephen reached the ledge, the creature was panting and slobbering froth from his massive jaws.

He climbed up just far enough to be out of the bear's reach. The roaring and growling made an awful noise in Stephen's ears. His only thought was a desire for this to be quickly over. He reached to his side and dislodged a large stone that seemed to weigh more than himself. With a struggle and a shaking in his lean arms, he raised the rock over his head and lunged it at the head of the angry bear. The rock bounced right off the bear's head, but the blow was more than effective. The bear tottered a bit and fell to the ground. Stephen jumped from the ledge, picked up the rock again with renewed strength, and gave a final blow to the bleeding head of the bear.

As the swirling in his head slowed to a ripple, his thoughts gathered in a prayer of thanksgiving to his Father for demonstrating His love to His child. His gratitude poured from his lips as the tears ran down his face.

As the other hunters made their way to the base of the rock cliff where Stephen now sat, there was a steady chant coming from them. Stephen recognized it as the tribal song reserved for those sacred moments that were so seldom seen anymore; the song went thus,

Blessed is he who receives the help of heaven.
Blessed more are they to whom he is sent.
Blessed are they to whom the Father of Spirits
visits through a willing vessel.
Blessed is he who receives the help of heaven.

Stephen erupted with praise as he recognized that the vision was revealing itself right before his eyes, even as humility covered him as a garment. But his praise caught in his throat as he thought about the attack and...Cutter!

Running back to the cliff where Cutter had been brought, he found him lying deadly still. Some feared him dead. Stephen uttered a silent prayer as sincere as his praise a moment earlier, as his hands quickly tended to his fallen comrade.

"Oh, Father of all Living, please don't let this one pass from among us. Favor him in this hour and restore life to him, and to your people as well. Let Your Joy chase away our sadness and Your Life drive out this death."

Cutter moaned softly under the touch of Stephen's gentle hand. Perhaps he will live! Relief showed on every face as they felt the tension lifting.

Stephen quickly gave direction for the preparation of items needed to help get Cutter back to the village. He tore strips from his own cloak to bind the severely injured, almost severed arm back alongside Cutter's body. He applied splints and more bandages to the herbal packing the others had already used to dress the wounds.

When at last Cutter had resumed steady breathing and had been positioned onto the travois, Stephen allowed himself some heartfelt praise and a few quiet tears of thanksgiving. Cutter would live. None that had been entrusted to him would be lost.

Homecoming

Once the hunters had been sent off and the damaged dwellings had been repaired, the elders assembled in the Place of Gatherings. The common belief was that it was time to relocate. Whenever the Horsemen became aware of the clan's location, the raids rarely happened only once.

It was also acknowledged that it would be necessary to place watchmen outside the perimeter of the village area and limit the amount of travel for those not in groups, and even they would have to be well armed and prepared to defend against an attack.

New Hope had been the clan's home for four cycles. It would not be easy to leave this time. It even seemed to some that the clan's pattern of life was changing. Every generation before had never lasted more than two full cycles in any one area, without the Horsemen bringing their destruction and inevitably, another move for the Peacemakers.

The growth season passed uneventfully for the clan, which actually had a reverse effect on them. They had increased their watchfulness and were basically always on the alert for a new raid. The Horsemen had not returned and though the tribe was glad, the inactivity was a torture of its own.

With Cutter badly wounded, Stephen thought it best to return to the village as soon as possible. The hunters had taken turns pulling the travois, two at a time. Cutter had been unconscious for some time, and Stephen was concerned about his heavy loss of blood. Stephen focused his whole being on holding the life of his friend before the Father of

Spirits. He could not bear the thought of returning to the village with the news of Cutter's death. He knew that would have been too much for him to endure and his heart grew increasingly heavy the farther they walked.

The young men who had been sent ahead as scouts could be seen in the distance moving towards the party. The hunter's were renewed by the sight, hoping that it was a sign that some of the clan had been encountered. A halt was called while the hunters waited for the scouts to return.

The scouts entered the grove where their brothers were resting and related with excitement the news that the perimeter guards posted around the village area had been seen no more than a quarter day's march ahead. The mood of the gathering brightened, but also brought to remembrance the condition the village was in at the time of their leaving. To know that full watch duties had been instituted upon the party's departure from the village brought a measure of peace, but the atmosphere did take on a noticeably different heaviness. They could only hope that there had been no further raids.

The hunters did the best they could to shake the dust from their garments and clean their weapons. After Stephen was sure that Cutter was comfortable, the party made their way back to the main path that would take them into the village and they set a steady, but quick pace.

The closer the party came to their much anticipated reunion to family and tribe, their heaviness was replaced with rising joy and expectancy in all but Stephen. He walked with head bowed, except when he glanced up to the harvest sky and uttered a prayer for his friend. The evening stars did not hold the same attraction they usually did for him; his whole world seemed clouded and subdued. He found himself slipping into a mood that was unfamiliar to him and he reminded himself to not lose hope. Hope, he knew, was all that he had.

As the party neared the village, it seemed as though the entire clan had come out to welcome them home! The hunters had seldom felt more loved and honored as they did at that moment. Even Stephen couldn't help but give in to the spirit of joy, as he glanced down to see Cutter trying to force himself up for a look. The cheers from the village had awakened him from his fitful sleep. He had regained consciousness shortly after leaving the grove, but had only done so for a moment before nodding back off to wherever he had found comfort for most of the day.

Stephen placed a hand on Cutter's good arm and told him to hold on just a little longer. He made some jest about there not being any of those poor little bears around here for him to wrestle with, and Cutter grimaced, as a chuckle escaped him, sending a sharp pain to his arm.

Something was happening between the two of them, and it was very good. The Father of Spirits was knitting their hearts together and they both recognized it.

The celebration was packed with such overflowing joy as to be almost intoxicating. The pent up frustrations of the growth season, which was normally the Peacemakers most active time, had found itself an outlet and the whole village was caught up in the merry making.

As for the hunters, they had all participated in the celebrations of previous hunts, but they had never been the guests of honor! And the way the girls looked at them now! This was certainly something new... and good.

Children of each family were full of questions and couldn't seem to stand still long enough for an answer. The parents were beaming with pride for their sons.... this was unbridled joy.

The village feasted on fresh bear meat, roasted over open spits that the women had fired upon hearing that the scouts had been seen earlier

that day. The news of the returning party had passed swiftly to eager
hearts. Fresh bread and herb sauces were added to the banquet table by
the young women who had been making preparations of their own for
the coming frost season. The men had brought honey mead from the
cooling caves. And around the fire was placed all the dried meat and
the huge piles of hides the hunters had brought with them as a sign of
thanksgiving and an offering in the sight of the Father of Spirits for His
goodness and provision.

The night was long and the celebration great, but weariness was
not far behind. Stephen, enjoying and always choosing solitude over
merriment, soon found an excuse to leave the festivities by calling on
Cutter to see that he was well. Quietly, he sought out the low hut near
the center of the village.

Cutter had been taken to the healing hut, where Stephen now stood
beside him. The wound seemed to be healing well enough and would
only require clean bandages and plenty of rest. Stephen whispered a
prayer, just loud enough for Cutter to hear, and Cutter nodded his head
in agreement, as Stephen turned to go. It had been a long day and they
both needed rest. There would be occasion for much time for them to
spend together in the coming days.

It was only one new moon before Cutter was well enough to be up
and about. He still wore a brace on his wounded arm, but Stephen had
him working a bow as soon as he could maintain a semblance of a grip.
Throwing the spear and using the lance were not so readily resumed,
but everything had its own time and Stephen was sure to keep Cutter
busy recuperating. They loved to be in one another's company and spent
endless pleasant times together. They never seemed to tire of walking
and talking together in the woods, by streams or just sitting on a hill
watching the sun set. The smallest acts held so much meaning for them
when they were shared with the other.

Stephen had begun sharing with Cutter a few of the many visions he had received and was almost shocked that Cutter wasn't overwhelmed by them! In fact, he not only found them believable, but embraced them whole-heartedly. Why, he was even anxious to hear more! For Stephen, life took on new meaning now that he had a friend. Joy had an outlet, at last.

Travels

When word came to Stephen that the elders had decided to relocate the clan, he was not surprised, he was actually a little relieved. He knew that as long as his people were afraid of the Horsemen, they would forever be subject to their torment. So, maybe it was better to just move on, rather than stay and be trampled under foot. One day...one day it would not be so.

New Hope held many memories for him, but he had little regard for anything this side of the Triall. He did not have to fight emotions, as the others of the clan did. Packing his meager belongings was an indifferent experience for him, much the same as he would have felt to simply go out and move an animal pen.

The one idea of leaving New Hope that did have some bearing on Stephen was the rumor that they may be moving south. That meant warmer weather, and warmer weather meant better fishing and more enjoyable walks in the evenings. These seemed to be the only activities that held Stephen's interest, because it was in these activities that he was usually alone and was able to have uninterrupted communion with His Creator. But he was aware of a certain, strange foreboding about any plans that would take the clan deeper into the wilderness of Cann.

Since returning from the hunt, Cutter had spent a lot of time with Stephen and he began accompanying him on his treks. Stephen was a little surprised to find that Cutter's presence did not hinder his communion. After a while, it even seemed that they were both enjoying a type of joint communion; in fact, because they were so closely united in heart, their communion with the Creator seemed to increase.

In the span of two new moons the village was ready to travel. They could have left far earlier, but that would have meant leaving the crops in the field, which was unthinkable. Vegetables and seeds required drying and much work was involved in their preparation for the frost season. It was determined that the dwellings and other structures would be left intact, in the event that the clan or any other travelers had need of it in the future. Even if the Horsemen returned and completely destroyed the village, the remains would still be of use to anyone requiring shelter.

In the cycle of Stephen's birth, the clan leader's life was cut short by a Horseman during another of their many raids. The responsibility of leadership then fell to the elders of the clan. The tribal pattern required that no certain one assumed leadership and likewise, no one inherited it. The position was attained only by the evidence of the Father's hand upon the one to whom the burden was given.

Dunn had explained to Stephen, not in way of slander, but honesty and in a matter-of-fact manner, that Standard, the fallen leader, had gradually stopped living up to his namesake. In the man's early years he had brought the Peacemakers much good through his ability to guide the clan in wisdom and love. However, it was recognized by the few of the clan who had continued to admonish Standard to return to the old paths, that his death was actually their Shepherd's act of mercy, for in removing Standard, He had not allowed them to be swept away with Standard's rebellion. But all of the elders did not hold to such train of thought and were supporters of Standard and his ways right up to the time of his death. It was the actions of these elders that Dunn had tried to prepare his son for. He knew that what they stood for would prove to be Stephen's greatest foe.

As the clan left New Hope, it was the prayer of Stephen's heart that the Father of Spirits would lead them not to some new village place, but to the homeland. He was so tired in his spirit. He had eyes only for the lands of Ability. That prayer remained to be answered.

The clan's travels brought them deeper into the Wilderness of Cann than any of them had ever dared to travel. The tribe settled in an area between two streams. One emptied into a large body of water, the other meandered on through the hill country for several days journey to the south.

The village was located in a well defensible position with multiple avenues of escape as well. The small streams provided much food. It was easy for the women to wash garments, and bathing in the warm waters was a blessing to the clan. The place was called Two Rivers and it was the best area that most of the Peacemakers had ever known. That may have been why the Horsemen did not allow them to reside there in peace for long.

Before the cycle's harvest season came, the clan was forced to move again. The raids were frequent and several of the clan lost their lives before the village was forsaken and the clan fled still further south. Another village was not built for many cycles, only season after season of walking, hunting, sleeping and... weeping. The further south the clan moved, the heavier their spirits became. And there seemed to be no relief in sight.

The present state of the tribe should have been a sign to those who had understanding among them, but even had they sounded an alarm, there were none to heed their call. The heart of the people had grown callused and there was no open vision among them.

It was in this state that the people found themselves short on water and their food rations low. Scouts had returned with news of a great body of water and high hills to the west less than a day's journey, where there was sure to be fertile soil and game a plenty. General indifference was the answer from the assembly as the elders brought what they felt would be good news. The tribe as a whole had lost the desire to hope. Had they known anything of the horrors of the Vale of Nott firsthand, they would have stoned the elders on the spot. To their misfortune, they were about to learn why so many that returned from Nott were hollow-eyed and devastated.

Bitter Waters of Nott

The clan had been traveling aimlessly for many days. The few who had brightened at the words given by the elders had lost even the little encouragement they had gained... burned out of them by the blazing sun.

It was the custom of the people to send the animals ahead with a small number of herdsmen to attend them. By mid-morning the last of the thirst-driven herd arrived at the body of water the scouts had reported seeing. The rest of the tribe came upon them while the sun was burning hot overhead, long after their last water skins had been drained.

Terror slowly registered as the elders were told the devastating news by the head herdsman that the beasts had refused the waters. Heedless of the threat, several of the younger herdsmen had splashed into the murky waters only to find its fetid stench clinging to their bodies as dung from a pit.

A low murmur made its way through the tired and desperate travelers as the news spread its way through the clan, and growing to a clamoring throng of voices. The elders looked to one another in a panicked glance as they sought to fix the blame elsewhere, their helplessness becoming evident to all.

The bellowing of the sheep and cattle echoed through the ears of Stephen and Cutter as they watched the wretched scene with compassion bordering pity. It seemed that the people were determined to be this way forever; moving from one catastrophe to another, the next worse than the one before.

In a rush of madness, a woman broke from the midst of the people and ran to the waters edge. Pushing all reason aside, she splashed the putrid liquid to her mouth, then, cupping her hands, drank down as much of the poison as she could before its effect took hold of her, wrenching her insides, twisting her with pain. She fell into the lake, a frenzy of flailing arms and legs. Before any could reach her, she was still. Only the waters around her rippled from the violence of her outburst.

Stephen and Cutter made their way to the waters edge. The woman, they noticed, was one who had once been found wandering the woods on the outside perimeter of the village. Upon questioning, none could rightly determine exactly what had happened to her. She only muttered bitterly, "Please, keep it away from me. Keep it away. It won't leave me!"

The life was gone from her and there was a certain awareness that whatever had once tormented her had fully laid claim to her as its rightful due. Her body was removed from the water and the elders gave orders for her to be buried away from the waters that had become her end.

The foreboding thought of their present situation brought the clan back to reality and the murmurs began anew. No amount of beseeching from the elders would still the clamoring crowd and the small children were becoming frightened.

Stephen looked about for his father and found him speaking in hushed tones to Teldig, son of the Chief Elder. His words could not be distinguished but his expression was one of displeasure. Teldig also seemed not pleased and Stephen tried to bring himself into their company without seeming to intrude on the conversation. If he had known how welcome he was in their midst he would have forgone the courtesy.

When their words slowed enough for him to interject a thought, he said, "Father, forgive my intrusion, but I believe I have seen."

"Speak freely, Stephen, as you know you may."

"Yes, you know you are ever welcome." Teldig added with a warming smile.

Stephen raised a finger to point towards the eastern sky. As the two men followed his gesture, he said, "Cutter and I have been noticing that there have been gulls coming and going on the eastern horizon. Why would there be gulls in the middle of this wasteland? Would it not be advisable to send a few men to investigate? I perceive that there may be a very good explanation over those foothills.

"Furthermore, I like not this bitter murmuring of the people. Sure destruction awaits the whole clan if we continue to speak thus against the Father of Spirits."

Dunn looked at his son with an affirming glance, then smiled as Teldig asked, "Is this not the answer to the prayer we have just offered?"

It was given to Stephen, Cutter and Teldig's son Jair to look to the source of the activity of the gulls. In the event that they found water, the three young men were given enough skins to ensure a ration for each member of the clan. The strongest mule was sent along as the three made off in the direction of the eastern foothills. Water or no water, Stephen was glad just to be out of midst of the complaining murmuring clan.

Their journey was not long and by the time the heat of the sun was being banished behind them by the Mountains of Nott, they topped the crest of the foothills. What welcomed them took their breath away.

The foothills kept to a tight oval, hiding all that was within from the outside world. A small trickle of sparking water streamed from beneath a large rock in the northern-most corner of the clearing within. They gazed out upon trees, flowers, and small animals scurrying at the sight of the four strange creatures violating their sanctuary. They tasted the fragrance of a gentle cool breeze, and fresh, never walked upon grassy meadows. The place was beautiful!

The thought of gathering water escaped them, and in one great burst of life they leapt down the slope and filled their lungs with the pure clear air. The only natural inclination was to run the full length and breadth of the meadows, drinking in the power of such unadulterated landscape. Mysteriously, all three found themselves drawn to the rock.

At first glance, it would have appeared that a small crevice at the base of the rock was the source of the stream. Further inspection brought more confusion. The rock was solidly lodged and no space permitted a crevice of any size. The water clearly trickled from the rock itself! What wonder was this? After circling the mass of stone and concluding that there was no answer to be established, the young men sat down and simply stared in disbelief.

As the people waited for the scouts to return, Dunn and a few of the other clansmen began to look to the guards posted on the outer reaches of the tribes resting place. There was a rising gut feeling among them that there was an enemy approaching. However, there seemed to be no cause of alarm at the various positions. Finally, the murmurs grew to an unbearable level. Several of the clan had broken out into actual scuffles over some trifling matter and the whole assembly teetered on the brink of complete anarchy.

In this time of outright devilish actions, an ominous rumbling sent a low moan of dismay through the gathering. The rumbling seemed to die a bit, but actually was bending into a low-pitched wail. With force the low wail became a scream and when it seemed it could not continue, it only gained force until most of the clan lay on the ground clutching their hands to their ears to drown out the dreadful sound.

First one, then two, then whole groups were making to their feet and running with all their might in the direction their young scouts had previously departed. The people were stumbling, fighting; tearing at anything in their path to get clear of whatever it was that was driving them. The herd of animals panicked at seeing such human degradation and stampeded as well.

Those who abstained from the murmuring rebellion watched in horror as the stampede of men and beast overcame the clan and sent them screaming from the foul lake. It was then that Dunn began to understand faintly that the source of their terror had come not from without, but from within. Their disobedience had taken on a tangible character and found expression in the form of unbridled fear of heart.

The further and faster the people ran, the closer and stronger the terrorizing noise came. It was not until they were breathless and stumbling to the ground, heaving in the dust, that they realized it was finally silent.

After exchanging glances of dismay and sorrow, the remaining clan members gathered the small children and straying animals that had been crushed underfoot or chased to the winds by the throng of madness, and made their way to where the tribe had finally ceased its headlong stampede. Shame and lingering fear were plain on every face, mixed with tears, dust and bruises. They were a pitiful looking lot.

Reproach could find no place in their hearts as the faithful came upon their tribe and realized the extent of the darkness in each heart. They knew full well that what they had witnessed was, in truth, the place of every heart when hardened in bitterness against the Father of Spirits. No, this was no time for judgment, but rather for the reaching out in healing and nourishment. The clan needed to see that in their worst time, He was still their greatest Friend. As they walked among their fallen brothers and sisters, in each of the faithful was the recognition that they truly did want to show His friendship. Not one of those in need turned from a helping hand.

The scouts were quite amazed to crest the hilltops to find the clan not half a league from the base of the foothills. With eager anticipation they made their way down the hill and, exchanging doubts and hopes, did their best to keep from running. They fell to silence and squashed any thought of danger.

The sight that met them was not what they had hoped to find. The moaning and crying in the clan's midst frightened the scouts and they dare not ask the question burning from within, until they could locate a reliable source of information.

Teldig caught their attention and they made their way to where he was bent over a couple of the older women of the tribe, doing the best he could to comfort and reassure them that everything was going to be all right.

Teldig motioned them off to the side where he could speak openly with them. He explained with fervor what had transpired in the short time since their departure, and described the ensuing stampede. The youths listened with disgust and sorrow interchanging and coloring each face. Stephen left the circle to find his family, Cutter followed close behind.

"Cutter, see to the water, as I look to your father and sister."

"I will, Stephen."

The clan slept safely, if fitfully, that night, under a star-filled sky. Stephen had chosen several men from the strongest of those who had not fallen prey to the spirit that had overcome the tribe. From these he had detailed a night watch, not so much to guard against outside enemies, rather so that every eye might rest upon at least one vigilant, armed sentinel. Having taken the first watch himself, Stephen lay gazing into the heavens barely aware that the sun was soon to find its place on the crest of those eastern foothills. Just before the first light of the coming dawn drew near, his eyes closed and he slipped peacefully under a gentle blanket of rest.

Bending Waters End

The following days passed uneventfully and the incident at the Bitter Waters of Nott, although unforgotten, were put behind them. The clan rested and regained their strength in the shadow of the foothills, later named "Thirst Slayer" in story and song.

Curiosity was high among the clan concerning what existed inside the hills, but the scouts, knowing the beauty of the place and its undefiled atmosphere, thought it wise to not announce their find. Surely, if these lands should be the kingdom of some grand lord, the man defiling them would be held accountable, even to the price of his own soul.

After several days recovery, the clan was, if not willing, at least ready to move on. No matter how much they dreaded traveling, all were aware that they could not remain in the open wasteland in which they now found themselves.

The clan made their way around the foothills and headed east. The Triall was eight days journey before them and they were fortunate to have collected sufficient water in their skins before leaving Thirst Slayer. Game became more plentiful with every sunrise and on the morning of the fifth day there remained none of the melancholy that had taken over the largest part of the clan.

The clan found themselves on the eighth day of their journey facing an area of long sandy beach where the river had flooded out many times leaving behind the perfect washing and bathing area. The waters ran slowly through many bends before reaching the site and gently quickened its pace about an arrow-shot down stream. The place became known as

Bending Waters End. The banks of the river above the chosen area were steep, the water clear during the dry season and the fish seemed oblivious to those who were stealthy with the spear. The hearts of the people were immediately attached to the place.

The clan rejoiced when it was told by the elders that a village would be raised. The Peacemakers had been journeying for six cycles with but little of that time spent in any one area. Everyone from the youngest fumbling hands to the gnarled and masterful hands of experience joined in the efforts to provide shelter in this blessed place.

The harvest season soon found them with a small crop, but the bountiful game more than made up for their lack; fresh meat and fish were never so plentiful on the tribe's tables. There were no complaints in the dwellings...yes dwellings! The women of the clan had not had dwellings in such a long time. Thanks was offered continually and the old ways seemed not so distant.

The time of snow passed and the coming of the flowers was at hand. Stephen would see his eighteenth cycle and rumor had it that there would be an important ceremony held before this year's Twelfth Cycle Hunt, which was the first such hunt in over five cycles. Speculation was rampant and Stephen noticed that many more looks were coming his way than normal. He tried to spend as much of his time alone as possible. There was always time for his family and the few who he found easy conversation with, and of course there was Cutter, but for the most part, he kept his own company.

The Chief Elder, Jaireth, rapped his ash cane against the base of the carved stone before him. The whispers of the assembly died away and he stood looking on them for a long moment. As he opened his mouth to speak, the words echoed through the village to every person gathered. He rehearsed to them the traditions of the clan concerning their allegiance to the Father of Spirits and to those He chose to raise up in their midst.

He shared with them the faithfulness of His mercies in delivering the people time and again; even in the times of the hardness of their hearts, He was ever faithful.

He reminded them of the old ways when Standard had been to the people a wise and true leader, and that not since his rebellion had the clan been given a leader. Glances were exchanged by knowing eyes around the gathering and most of them crossed Stephen's face more than once. He remained steady under the scrutiny and tried to maintain his focus on Jaireth.

Before Jaireth had finished his speech, Stephen's thoughts had wandered to that place they often did, and he found himself again in the homelands of Ability. The longings caused his heart to swell as Cutter nudge him with his elbow.

Jaireth was looking at him, as was the whole clan; Cutter whispered, "He's waiting for you. Didn't you hear him, Stephen? Go ahead."

After making his way forward, Stephen knelt before the Chief Elder as he indicated with his ashen cane. The other elders who had been standing to the side now gathered round and each placed a hand on Stephen. Jaireth produced a clay vial from beneath his tunic and broke the seal. The sweet smell of olive and rose permeated the air and the elders began first to whisper a quiet chant that grew to a low melodic verse unrecognizable to Stephen.

The verse ended just as he seemed to be picking up some of the repeated syllables. The elders fell away to leave Jaireth, one hand on Stephen's head and the other holding the vial over him. He poured the contents out over Stephen and allowed the oil to run down the length of his body. The oil was warm and very pleasing to the senses and brought forth a memory in which the Father of Spirits had been so near that it seemed Stephen was immersed in warm oil, just as he was today.

Jaireth held out the vial, an elder took it from him and replaced it with the Staff of the Peacemakers.

The staff was a long rod made of red oak, carved by one of the fathers of the homeland. Upon the top of the staff was embedded an emerald of the finest quality, in which it was said in earlier days, the whole of the world could be viewed by looking into the stone. Down the length of one side of the staff were rows of pure gold inlaid with ivory cut in the shape of lambs. On the other side were sculptured marble eagles. The lamb was significant of the innocence and utter dependence upon the Shepherd; the eagle represented the beauty and freedom of a people who would live their lives abandoned to their Creator and none other.

Jaireth touched the staff to the crown of Stephen's bowed head and asked him to stand. Stephen, dizzy from the ceremonies and emotions clouding his vision, faltered a moment, gathered his strength and senses and rose from his kneeling position. He was fully head and shoulders above Jaireth, and clearly the tallest member of the clan. He made for a very suitable leader; his physical aspects mirrored images of the inner man the clan had come to respect and love.

Stephen turned to stand beside Jaireth. Jaireth motioned him to the elevated chiseled stone and handed him the staff. Stephen accepted the token of tribal leadership and stepped upon the stone. Despite being used to his own abnormal height, Stephen felt the awkwardness of being elevated unnaturally above his fellow clan members. He stepped off the stone and, casting a sidelong glance at his father, addressed the people, "Brothers and sisters, my kinsmen, I stand before you today as your leader, but I remain your brother. I hold this staff only because the Father of Spirits has desired it to be so. I call you to witness this day that I have neither sought nor desired this staff. Knowing that it is by His design that it has fallen to me to hold it, I shall hold it faithfully and willingly to the day it is removed from my hand by He who gave it."

As his words settled upon the tribe, the song of dedication rose and soon reverberated throughout the village. His heart rose with it as tears streaked his face.

Aieda looked on with both joy and sadness. His mother had watched him grow and saw how the people had truly taken to him, but she often wondered if it were out of love or desperation. To see them turn on him would be too much for her gentle heart to endure and she did not desire to see her son hurt. She also knew that her son was in the care of the Great Shepherd. In this was her only peace.

Dunn was aware of Aieda's feelings and held her hand in his and gave her a soft kiss on the cheek. He had his own reservations about the adoration and praise being lauded on his firstborn, but he kept his counsel to himself. This was to be a day of celebration and he had no desire to cast doubt on the future of the clan.

As the song died away, Stephen opened his eyes and held the staff high. When silence replaced the clapping and shouting, Stephen lowered the staff and shared his heart with the people. The elders shuffled their feet as with his first words he explained that he intended to bring the clan across the Triall and back to Ability before the next planting season. A rumble of differing opinions made its way through the assembly. When he sensed their attention re-focus upon himself, he waited until there was again complete silence. When he finally spoke, it was from the abundance of the vision that gave him reason to continue and had carried him throughout the years in hope. The excitement exuding from him seemed to catch like a hot flame on a thatch roof and soon the whole gathering was spellbound with the words that went straight from his mouth to their hearts. He spoke long into the evening and none were the worse for it.

Except for the news of his plans to cross the Triall, all went well. The elders were uncertain if they may have been a bit presumptuous, now that his mind was known, yet, the thing was done and now they would have to wait and see the fruit of it.

Stephen awoke the next morning feeling spent. He had spoken long and the oil of the Spirit of Heaven had rested upon him as he spoke. He silently gave thanks and rose to make his way down to the sandy beach to freshen himself before his morning meal.

As he made his way to the water, a very pleasant sight interrupted his thoughts. Shayla, Cutter's younger sister, (wasn't she just a child the last time he saw her?) was coming from the washing area with a bundle of cooking utensils. Stephen started to greet her, but his voice betrayed him as his words stumbled and his feet completed the act of treachery by tripping over a rock, his face turning crimson red. Shayla giggled as her stride carried her gracefully up the hill. Stephen, still sprawled on the sandy beach, tried to understand the feelings coursing through him.

Stephen had frequently been viewed as a loner, because of his tendency to withdraw, yet in truth he truly loved the people of the clan and in his own heart could never set himself apart from them. He did not desire their adulation and did not want to be the focus of the people's attention, and because of this he often chose to walk alone. The turmoil within Stephen was how to continue to be an example to the clan and lead them on higher paths without drawing attention to himself. All along he had know he was to be a leader...yet how, without dragging this people behind him, could he ever accomplish this, short of a miracle? It would take at least a miracle, he mused.

But Shayla...somehow Stephen knew that this girl saw right through his confusion and was not deceived in any way about him. It was, at one and the same time, both disconcerting and very comforting. "Ha, Shayla, perhaps you have seen my heart!" He washed, tried to regain his composure and made his way to his father's dwelling for a welcome meal.

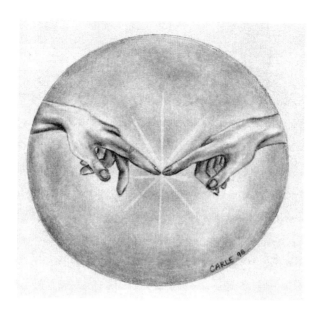

Joining

She hadn't noticed his gaze upon her as she had made her way to the village hall. The two youngsters she prodded along kept her full attention and she seemed quite content that it was so. He tried to pull his eyes from her but it was useless. He was fully captivated by her.

Shayla's long, light brown hair was pulled back and wrapped in a colorful garment that had been carefully dyed from an assortment of berries she had discovered growing near the river's bank. The girlish freckles from her youth were fading and her complexion was darkening under the new sun to a smooth reddish brown that gave her uncommon green eyes an extra twinkle as the light touched upon her face. Her high cheekbones and slender nose gave her lineage away and her resemblance to her older brother Cutter brought a smile to Stephen. She would enter her seventeenth cycle this harvest season. The light that was in her was growing more radiant now than ever and it was especially evident to Stephen.

As he looked on the three of them now, the thoughts of the raid that left the children orphaned and thrust into Shayla's care burst upon him anew.

It had been an extremely quiet night. but that was nothing new. The winds had not blown for days and there had been no rain for weeks. The clan traveled almost nonstop. The elders declared camp in the first place that appeared to offer hope of rejuvenation and fresh water. A small spring bubbled from a rocky outcrop, feeding a glen of walnut and maple trees. The clan took a breath of relief and began erecting the temporary tent-like structures that were used for their shelter when they would not be staying in an area long enough to establish dwellings.

Besides finding the spring, the day had been relatively uneventful. Stephen rested momentarily, with his thoughts first converging then scattering one another over and again. He could sense the fleeting happiness of the clan. To the people, having water and shelter were as far as they could see. But Stephen had a deep foreboding that told him something hung just out of sight...waiting, watching, and looking for an opportunity to move on an unsuspecting prey.

It was then that he had stirred to check on the outposts. There were no actual signs of distress that one could see. He felt foolish as he approached each new station to find all in order, his tribe-brothers giving him a questioning glance. Still, in his heart, he knew the turmoil within him was real and he must remain alert.

On his way back to his shelter, he had recalled a huge walnut tree in the glen that spread its branches wide and decided to watch the sun sink behind the mountains of Nott from there. He was almost persuaded that all was well when he heard that unforgettable sound.

His head came up to see four horsemen corralling a group of women and their young as the day's washing was being done. The harrowing screams and the clanging of shield against sword brought cries of dread from the helpless women and children.

Harden, the husband and father of three who were at the spring, came running to the aid of his family. A horseman, not seeing him, though it mattered little, turned his mount to circle the gathered prey and Harden met his end beneath the battle trained hooves of the stallion. His wife, Rena, seeing her husband slain before her eyes, in a frenzy of anguish, threw herself upon the horseman, finding her own doom at the point of his sword.

Stephen ran to their aid, amazed to see another clansman had run into the cluster of animals, men and steel, brandishing a lance and a covering of some kind. The horsemen had not noticed him and he had managed to make his way practically under them. He raised a whooping cry and began waving the covering, the hide of a wolf, before the nearest horse. As the horse reared over his head, he thrust the lance with all his strength into the breast of the beast. Not waiting to see the result of his actions, he caught the next with lightning speed, and the next until he had routed all four horsemen. Their horses limping and skittish with pain, the Giant Horsemen urged their mounts away and were gone, before the wolf-man could claim their blood as well.

As Stephen approached and clapped the back of the other clansman, his shock overwhelmed him. The wolf pelt fell off to reveal the long brown hair of a woman, and as she turned, the fierce look in her green eyes melted to compassion as she spotted the now-orphaned children. Shayla! What glorious courage! What holiness and absence of fear! And from one so unsuspecting! He could not contain the joy that flooded his heart as he realized that this was the first time he had seen such a feat from another of the clan and that from Shayla!

His joy was full and only overshadowed by the pain that resulted from the loss of two clan members. Then his heart also turned to the two small children huddled in grief over their fallen parents. It was then that Shayla proved herself more valiant still.

Then and there she took upon herself the responsibility of the two children. There was never a question whether there would have been one more qualified to raise them. There were no other volunteers.

They had been only babes when the raid occurred, but not too young to know the pain of loss. Their sorrow was not evidenced now. In the short time since, Shayla had so clearly cherished them that the pain they had known was enveloped by her unfailing love. Even the other women, although in their fears they had seldom included her because of her radiant confidence and self-composure, had commented on how naturally she had taken up the burden, unappointed, save by the conviction of her own heart.

Stephen had been occupied in deep contemplation for days and Cutter had noticed his disposition early.

"How does my Chief come to sit upon a rock looking so distraught when he should be instructing young ambitious warriors or apportioning justice for his clansmen, or any of ten other duties?" Stephen eyed him curiously and dismissed his friend's humor with a wave of his hand. Cutter laughed out loud. "Come now, what could hold such sway over my brother and Chief Warrior? The whole tribe is in a whirl of joy and fullness of life and their leader sits atop his perch with the whole of the world on his shoulders. Is there no mirth for you, my friend? Let us get ourselves down to the stream for a good swim. It may be that the cool water will clear the melancholy from your bones. Maybe all the excitement has overcome you."

Stephen had not so much as noticed that his friend's discourse had gone on past his initial jest and caught only this last. "Overcome me? Whatever have you been rattling on about?"

"Look, Stephen, you have been sitting here like this far too long. Forgive me my untimely humor, but I care only that my friend's company is stolen from me by some errant thought. Maybe I too would join him on his journey. It is more than obvious that something is weighing heavily upon you. If you please, I would hear the matter."

Stephen was reluctant to acknowledge the truth of Cutter's statement, but was already growing irritated by his badgering, as innocent as it was. "I don't know what has gotten into me, Cutter. I seem to have lost my wits to the will of another. My whole being seems entangled in a web of longing for her, yet I know nothing of these matters. I feel absolutely foolish for my longings, my thoughts and my actions. And even still, she need but speak her request and it would be my heart's command."

Cutter appeared confounded by the revelation, not conceding that he already knew his sister to be the object of his friend's dilemma, enjoying the game of drawing Stephen out into a field of play. Having become the best of friends, Cutter had come to view Stephen's propensity for deep thought as a thing to be assailed, not out of spite, but simply as a means to engage Stephen on a mock battlefield, and received great pleasure in doing so!

A game of cat and mouse followed and Stephen became more agitated for allowing himself to be coerced into speaking forth the very thing he had attempted to reason away, thus giving it life and reinforcing its presence in his heart. He would have kicked himself, had he not found the ache deep within him abating even as he spoke to his friend.

"You mean to tell me that is all it is? Not some great undertaking that will require a full warriors delegation, or the calling of a tribal gathering for consultation, nor a journey to the lands of cold Faate for the capturing of the Ice Mother's children?" Cutter allowed a sheepish grin to pass over him and continued his assessment of the situation. "Stephen, Shayla grows weary with your worrying." This last caught Stephen's full attention.

"What are you saying? Why do you speak to me of your sister?"

"Do you deny that she is the reason for your mournful state? Do you wish me to believe you are not aware that this whole village has been talking of nothing else for days? And will you keep her waiting until the dowry is moth eaten and corrupted before it is to be accepted? Open your eyes friend! You have kept the girl waiting long enough."

"You mean to tell me that you already knew about this and said nothing?"

"I was under oath, brother; she could not make her desire known. Her honor demands that she remain hidden until her beloved calls on her. In remaining honor-bound, she would have waited forever. I would say her patience has yielded a bountiful harvest!"

Cutter's words brought a silence over Stephen and after some time he looked up from the dust he had been drawing in with a stick. "I suppose I have been very foolish. I am humbled by such patience. She is a worthy princess, is she not?"

Cutter let this last pass without comment. "Go see her, she knows your struggle. She has desired to comfort you, but she could not. She will be relieved that you have come through."

Cutter gave his friend no mercy as he practically ushered him off in the direction where he knew Shayla to be waiting near the riverbank. With a burst of joyous laughter, he slapped Stephen on the back as his salutation sent his friend on his way.

He found her near the water's edge, gathering berries, the evening sun sending scattering hues of gold, purple and bronze ripples of light over the water behind her. He had never beheld such combined beauty and the thought crossed his mind that a goddess stood before him. He stood there watching her for some time, drinking in her presence, until she looked up to see him.

She said nothing. They watched one another for a long moment and strained to cause it to last as long as possible. All of the anxiety he had previously experienced seemed to have melted away as he looked into her cool green eyes and allowed them to persuade him of her love.

He came closer and sat beside the basket at her feet. He spread his cloak out for her and she sat down. She offered him a few of the delicious berries she had collected. When he turned down the offer, she took a few up and said, "They are very good. This cycle has been very productive. Never have the berries been so sweet...or so juicy!" With this last, she leaned over and stuck several large berries into his mouth, smearing the luscious juice over him. Before he could regain his composure, she was gone, vanished!

He wiped the dripping fruit from his face and called to her. "Shayla? Do not go. Wait!" He stood to pursue her, looking up the trail to where he thought she had run. A rustling in the brush caused him to turn. As he looked around, a gentle nudge took his balance from him. Grasping for something to hold to, he caught hold of her arm and both of them went splashing into the river.

Her rapturous laughter caught his ear as he came to the surface and he was overcome by her joy and the innocence that was so naturally hers. Stephen too began laughing and the sound of their voices together in mirth was music to the air. The birds and all the creatures of the wilderness seemed to have joined in the frolic and a song of nature burst forth. The melody of laughter ascended from the rippling water and the trees echoed with their joy.

They swam in the cool waters and enjoyed the rest of the day together. Their joy was full and there could be no doubt in either of them that they were truly meant for one another, and that there would be many such days to be shared together in the future.

The shaded grove overlooked the lazy, sandy stretch of beach to the south. The west side opened to look out over the open country of Cann. The east side dropped sharply to the rocky cliffs of the Triall, the north made impassable by a wall of thistles and briers.

Stephen and Shalya had begun spending their free time here and this is where they found themselves on a particular day. Stephen was dropping petals from freshly picked wildflowers over Shayla, allowing them to form a graceful crown over her shining brown hair. She had stopped wearing it bound up now that there was someone to admire and enjoy its beauty.

As his last petal touched down upon her regal crown, he rose from reclining on his elbow to kneel before her. Taking her hand in his own and looking deep into those gleaming green eyes, he said, "I would speak a word to my lady." Shayla laughed out loud and waved him away.

He reclaimed her hand and persisted, "I do not jest, Shayla. Please hear me." His eyes pleading, speaking the depth that his words could not. "I love you. It is no secret. I have openly shown you my heart. I would pledge myself to you, should you wish to have me. I would promise to always love, protect and provide for you. I will be a shield against your enemies and a tower of safety for you to run to. No burden will be too heavy as we bear it together. I will care for you as my own soul. Even now, I feel as though you are already part of me. Will you accept my pledge and pledge to me as well, Shayla?'

She had not expected it, but neither was she surprised. No, she had not yet considered their pledging, but it came so naturally that she did not take time to decide. What was to decide? Had she not already given him her heart? She was finding greater fulfillment in his presence everyday. Of coarse she would pledge to him! What else was there for them but to pledge?

Her softly spoken words were everything that Stephen had ever hoped to hear from her. "Stephen, I pledge to you freely, willingly and joyfully, for in truth I have loved you since ever I can remember. Father of Spirits be praised, for He has revealed you to me, and in you I see Him. Lead, for I will surely follow."

Stephen and Shayla spent every free moment together, their love for one another flourishing even as the season gave forth their increase. The clan seemed to receive life from the growing affection between the two of them. As the village began the gathering in of the crops, it was announced that there would be a joining between the two immediately following the harvest. It seemed there would be no end to the rejoicing the news brought. The work was over and done before anyone wearied and the village began to buzz with the joining preparations.

Stephen was adapting well to the cloak of responsibility that had fallen to him and he was growing stronger both in body and spirit. It was at this time that his sight began to strengthen, his vision into that other realm giving greater light. Shayla too, was changing, both inwardly and outwardly, her womanly virtue, her tenderness and her queenly ways captivating every person found fortunate enough to engage her in a moment's conversation. They were beautiful together and the people of the village were hopeful for what the coming joining of two such blessed souls might mean for the clan.

Stephen and Shayla were joined on a beautiful day with a gentle breeze blowing lightly across the Triall River, bringing with it the fragrances from the fields of Ability. Could this have been a sign? If it was, it was not wasted on Stephen; he was very much aware of it.

It seemed only right that their joining should take place in the grove where they had come to spend so much of their time. The joining ceremonies were not remarkable. All knew that the couple to be joined had already become one in heart and now simply were being joined in body as well. Their pledged vows declared publicly, they would now together inhabit a dwelling already fruitful with the inclusion of the orphans who joyfully received their new "parents."

Thus the harvest ended to bring forth the festivals and celebration of the greatest merrymaking the Peacemakers had know this side of the Triall River. And the celebration was great! Ah, what a season! Let the cold snows come. All was prepared. Nothing could dampen the warmth that filled every hearth. The dwellings overflowed with goodness and happiness and it was no wonder there were more births the following growth season than ever before. The fruitful harvest spilled over into the very lives of the clan! Stephen and Shayla were one of the many couples to welcome new life into their hearth the following cycle. Thus began their journey together, and blessed it was.

Shayle

The morning came with a red dawn and Stephen's mood fairly matched the day. Shayla had been laboring since dusk the night before, pale with exhaustion, strength coming only in spasms; the midwife did her best to keep the pacing husband out of sight. Dunn had finally been enlisted to usher Stephen away from the dwelling and hopefully even direct his thoughts elsewhere. Stephen proved a worthy opponent, but gave in to his father in the end.

By mid-morning, the whole tribe was aware of the prolonged labor and had gathered near the hut to know the outcome of the matter. This certainly did not help Stephen's disposition when he and Dunn returned from the clan's fish traps. The whole assembly went scattering as he walked among them with steely eyes fixed unswervingly at the gawkers and bystanders.

Dunn looked on and simply tried to keep a straight face. He could tell Stephen meant to harm no one, but he could also see that his son was very serious and would yield no ground, and none in his path believed he would either. In this they were correct.

Before he could make his way again to the dwelling entrance, a wail went forth from inside sending a chill up the back of all within earshot. Stephen forced his way through to where Shayla lay writhing and screaming, the midwife pushing Stephen back, speaking instructions to Shayla and warnings to Stephen at the same time.

He found himself a place in the corner and knelt to pray. His prayers covered the two women and his forthcoming child. He assaulted the heavens from his place on the floor and would not relent. His fervent pleas prevailed and as Shayla gave a final ear-shattering scream, her voice was joined with the rising yell of a strong-winded, beautifully formed male child.

As the babe was laid upon her breast, tears of joy replaced those of pain as she began to laugh with the prospect of life; life new-formed and brought forth through much pain, yet rewarded with unmeasureable ecstasy. The babe's eyes sparkled with life and his golden wavy locks gave him the aura of an angel. "A man-child, Stephen! Do you see him! Your son, behold your son!" Her voice weak and hoarse, she called to her husband, through laughter and tears.

She need not waste her breath. He was there and his joy was at least as strong as her own. He had feared losing both wife and child, knowing the dangers of such prolonged labor. Of a truth, this morning's vigil had not been his first. He had spent untold hours on countless days crying out to the Father of Spirits to be graceful in the saving of wife and child.

After the child had been cleaned and nursed, Shayla having regained enough strength to endure momentarily parting with her new gift, Stephen had taken the child out to present him to the clan. As they gathered around for a look at this remarkable child, he told them:

"Behold! I set before you today a great one. He shall grow to be wise in the way of his creator. He shall not heed the words of men nor bend to their traditions. His life shall not be his own, but wholly given to the purpose of the Father of Spirits. He shall ever be taught to hear the Voice that calls from Heaven and his prayers shall be as promises from above. He shall be called Shayle, for he shall kindle fire like a flint and his resolve shall be as stone.

"Mark you well, for this birth marks for us the beginning

of our departing from this cursed land. Prepare your hearts and make straight paths for your feet. Before the next moon, we cross the Triall into Ability."

The winter had been relatively quiet, no raids and the weather more than gentle. A few days after Shayle's birth, this was all brought to an end.

Stephen had been running a few traps near the grove where he and Shayla had been joined, when a runner stumbled up to him, his breath coming in gasps. Stephen steadied the youth and offered him water from his water skin. The youth pushed aside the skin and told of his errand. "I have just come from the southern watch post. There are Horsemen approaching up the bank of the Triall and it seems they are heading straight for the village. It cannot be said if they know of our presence, but they will soon enough."

"How many are there, Dunig?"

"At least ten, not more than twenty. They remain among the trees and their number cannot easily be assessed."

"Gather the strong among us and have them await me at the southern edge of the village. Have all the others remain in their dwellings; and tell them to pray. I will meet you when I am able."

After seeing Dunig crest the hill to the village, Stephen looked heavenward as his first means of preparation and cried out for protection and wisdom. His petition made, he arose and ran to see that his wife and son were safe, then made his way to the banks of the Triall. Once there, he loosed the boats, which were small craft used for running the fishing nets, and sent them gliding down the softly rolling water. He then placed in the water the empty cooking pots that had been left at the washing area on the sandy bank, careful to be sure they remained afloat. After surveying his work, he ran down stream to where the people had gathered.

As he looked over their expectant, but still fearful faces, he gathered his strength and addressed them. "We will stand as one against our enemy today." His declaration brought a rumble of shock and dismay over the people, who had expected to flee. He allowed the murmuring to quiet and continued. "All the males among us are to climb the trees along the water's edge. Each one of you take up as many stones as you are able to carry. The women will form a line a bow's length apart, hidden along the woods opposite the river's bank; each gathering to her a limb as large as she can wield. In this way, we will form a walkway the Horsemen will regret having treaded upon.

"I have already created a diversion and their attention will be on the water as they approach us. As the horses enter our midst, at my signal, the men will throw their stones into the water. The women are to lift up a victory shout and charge the horses with their upraised branches. Do not faint or be dismayed, for the Lord of the Battle has given you the victory today and from this day forth, if you will but obey!"

So saying, Stephen turned and ran down stream, leaving his clan-brothers and clan-sisters looking after him. Knowing their delay would only serve their destruction, they made fast to do as they had been instructed. And as they did so, faith rose up within every heart. They began to hope. Stephen prayed for them as he ran and could only hope they would respond. His hope was well placed. Courage mounted up in each of them and had they been armed warriors their valor could not have been greater, for they were clothed upon with the majesty of their Creator that day. The battle was before them and glory was soon to be had.

Stephen spotted the raucous band laughing their coarse jests to one another and cursing the gods of earth and sky. Their stench preceded them and he could hardly believe the human race could sink so low. He eyed the water of the Triall and saw his diversion floating by. He hefted one great rock, then another into the river, making sure they made a great splash and plenty of noise.

Certain that his plan was well set, he made his way up from the bank and into the woods. Circling around, he came behind the horsemen, who after seeing the empty boats and floating pots, grinned in anticipation of the thought of someone's obvious misfortune. Making their way cautiously up the bank, they thought to plunder some unsuspecting travelers floundering in the waters of the Triall.

As the Giant Horsemen came into the trap, their hearts were lifted up within them and their pride caused them to stumble, for they were looking to cause trouble and were not looking for trouble to find them. Stephen appeared behind the Horsemen to alert his clansmen to action. Each man let fly his stone at Stephen's signal and at the sound of many rocks bursting the tranquil rivers edge, the horses reared. At this, the women as one, leapt from their hiding to brandish their branches and let forth a deafening scream sufficient to raise the hair on one's back. And they did not yield. They drove the cowering beasts into the very waters of the river! The shock on the face of each Horseman! To see that look on the face of one's enemy, what a sight to behold! It is joy unspeakable to stand against your enemy and see him flee as a scalded hound!

Stephen had brought with him an armful of rocks. As soon as the horses reared, he began stoning them with all his might. The other clan members saw this and followed suit, and the Horsemen went down in a barrage of rocks. Soon the waters became gentle ripples once again and the enemy was no more. The Clan had fought against their enemies and had prevailed! Many voices raised in celebration. "Glory to the Watcher of Souls!" "You have delivered your people with a Sure Hand!" "Let Your light shine ever upon us!"

Thus began the time of flowers. Great was the rejoicing in the village of the Peacemakers. Soon all were remembering Stephen's words at the birthing of his son, as well as those when he received the Staff. Could this be that story which was said only in whispers? Would the enemies of the people finally be routed and their own namesake honored once again? Could it be that hope and faith might again find a place at their hearths, as in the times of old?

It was to this that Stephen knew he had been born. It was nigh at hand and he tasted it in every breath of air he breathed, he could smell it on the morning breeze, he could see it in dawn's first light. It reverberated within him and echoed through the hills. Deliverance, sweet and pure. The lands of Ability were within his grasp and he could hardly wait!

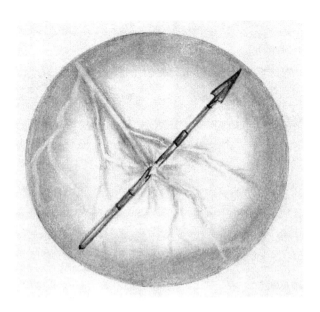

The Staff-Stone

"Father, I am looking for something. Have you ever looked for something that you could not name?" Stephen looked every bit as perplexed as he sounded, coming near to where Dunn was sitting, working the edge of a new knife he had been toiling over for several days.

Dunn, knowing the manner of speech his son was prone to use when in deep contemplation, did not answer right away, choosing rather to allow Stephen to speak his heart. He allowed a thought to linger that caused him to wonder at how much he truly loved this young man who had brought him honor such as a father was seldom worthy.

Stephen sat down at his father's feet and continued, "Father, tell me the mystery of the Staff-Stone."

Dunn was caught off guard by the question, but allowed his attention to remain on the knife in his lap, while he gathered his thoughts and decided how best to answer. Finally he decided to test his son's discernment.

"You know all the legends concerning the Staff, Stephen. If we are to speak of mysteries, why can we not talk of why your new nets have yielded us no supper?"

Stephen's nose wrinkled at his father's jesting and defensively countered that he was not to be responsible for the lack of cooperation he was receiving from the weather. The recent cold had turned the fish down-stream and it seemed they wanted nothing to do with his nets.

"I will not be put off by your attempts at luring me from my question. So, tell me of the Stone, please."

Dunn seeing that Stephen was intent on an answer, surrendered a measure.

"What gives you the idea that there is any mystery, as you say there is?"

"I have seen..." Stephen fumbled for the words that seemed to escape him, then continued in a thoughtful manner, "I did not see what the Staff-Stone was in days past. I saw rather what it is not. I saw a void. The Stone seems to be missing something it once was, and yet I saw also what it shall be. Does any of that make sense, Father?"

"You have both seen and spoken well, Stephen. The Stone is not what it has been and indeed shall never be that again. It does have a future and what has been foretold in ages long ago, shall be."

"Tell me what these things mean, Father."

Dunn laid his knife aside and stood to stretch the stiffness from his limbs and said, "Come, let's walk by the stream."

As they made their way down to the path that led along the bank of the gently rolling water, Stephen was barely at peace as he awaited Dunn's explanation.

"The Staff was made many, many cycles ago. When our People

were in Ability, things were very different. We knew Him who orders all things and His desire was the only object of our existence. We were recognized, not because of who we were as a people, but because of His presence in our midst. Things, as I said, were very different.

"In that time, the Stone was alive! Do you hear me, Stephen?" Dunn's excitement stimulated something in Stephen. Maybe he should have asked about the Stone sooner!

Dunn continued his story. "The purpose of the Stone was for guidance and witness to the Truth. The Stone lived and as the People closely followed the One who had kept them by His own power; the Stone was a living testimony to their being accepted and loved.

"But we were only accepted as long as we continued to believe the faithfulness of Him who had freely accepted us. The day came when we no longer embraced Him and our desires were placed elsewhere. The light of the Staff-Stone began to fade, and as it did, there were those who claimed it was evidence that His desire for His People had faded. We blamed our unfaithfulness on the One who had the power to love those who are truly unlovely. In our continual cold indifference to His love, we extinguished the fire of the Stone.

"On the final day that the last flickering light of the Stone ebbed, the Sage of the Staff stood before the people and spoke what were to be his last words. But they were words that proved to be eternal, for he spoke by the Father of Spirits. His words froze the heart of those who stood before him, and nearly everyone since has remained frozen. These same words will one day melt the hearts of ice.

"Mark the foretelling well Son, for I perceive that you have a part in its fulfillment. Mysteries are not for enticement, nor amusement. There is a purpose to all things."

"Father, I do not wish to be impatient, but by the time you tell me the foretelling it may well have been fulfilled already", Stephen said with a sly smile.

His father huffed and straightened for a steady gaze at his son, who in Dunn's estimation, had become a pleasantly handsome young man. Impatient though he was, Dunn loved him intensely.

"Though you do not esteem the finer points of the bard's art, I suppose your directness will account for something someday!"

After they had both had a good laugh of it, their mood took on a different nature and Dunn continued his story, his words not more than a whisper, "Hear again the words of Jared, Sage of the Staff, 'I stand as witness against you today. You have taken the Life of the Stone and She shall shine to you no longer. Because you have despised Her light, She is taken from you; She shall come to a people who do not know Her, and they shall love Her. This day, you have heard my words, and hereafter, you shall hear them no longer. Nor shall another speak to you the words of this Life. You shall look among yourselves for one who will bring them, as you shall look afar, yet you shall have them not. Until the day that One shall arise from among you who shall come forth as a flickering flame of righteousness and the Stone shall live again in His presence!'"

Dunn allowed the words to linger in the air a moment before going on. He could not read the expression on Stephen's face and tried to be sure he did not rush into his explanation and chase away the thoughts his son may be seeing in some new light. Carefully, he went on.

"The Sage gave up the ghost, while the people mocked his final words. As he fell asleep, tears of sorrow from too few spilled to the ground. The only solace for his departing spirit being that there remained a small, but faithful remnant. The Last Sage was gone and with his spirit went the last waning light of the Stone. The Staff-Stone grew dark. The Sage was dead. The People lost both their Light and Intercessor in one day.

"It was a very dark time for our people. The darkness has been with us for an ever-long time. We have tried to regain a semblance of the affection for the Father of Spirits that marked and set apart our forefathers, but we have such a long distance to travel, which lies yet ahead.

"Stephen, I am so very tired. I have waited so long to see us, as a People, look for His presence in our midst. I despair of waiting for that day." The silence left by the absence of his father's voice alarmed Stephen. He felt as though he should be holding his father, as though somehow their places were reversed by some unnatural act of nature. His father was as his own child, lonely and hurt in an ugly world of violent acts and turbulent spirits.

Stephen looked into his father's eyes and saw love, as though it had been left for many days unattended, aching and beseeching to be rescued.

"Surely, you do not believe that I will revive the light of the Staff-Stone?"

The words came from Stephen's mouth with an edge of sarcasm. He did not mean them as a reproach. He was dismayed that he should feel it necessary to ask such a question. After all, they were speaking of the Stone of the Staff!

Dunn held his counsel until he was sure that Stephen himself had plenty of time to consider all that had been said. They had come to a bend in the small stream and Dunn motioned for them to return up the path from whence they had come.

"I do not believe any man will revive the Stone. The Stone will be revived as a witness to the presence of the Father of Spirits in the midst of those to whom He shall reveal Himself. He will send one who will be instrumental in showing us the Way. I do not say that shall be you, Stephen. I only say what I know. And this is what I know: I know you have seen what many have failed to, and you have a heart that is hungry for him who is our Bread. I know that you will be used by His hand. How that shall play out remains to be seen. I only hope that I am allowed to live long enough to see it."

The Crossing

Stephen lay on the ground, his head buried in his hands, his prayers ascending to his Creator. He had labored there all night. As the dawn broke over the Triall, the grove became alive with the sparkles of cascading alight, falling on the fresh dew as a rainbow of multifaceted colors. The grove resembled a garden of jewels, and Stephen lay sprawled in the middle of this display of nature as though he were the center stone; the events of his life finally coming together much as this simple scene revealed. As he ended his petition, he heard that voice he had come to recognize so well. And this is what he heard;

"My child, you are my beloved and I have kept you with an everlasting love. You have been bought forth for My cause and were never to be as others. You were mine from the womb and to this day have I sustained you for My purpose.

"Do not fear, nor be anxious about tomorrow. I have set at hand that which you require for today. I will bring my people back to the lands I gave them from the beginning, but this is not My chief desire. A people that recognize Me as their Dwelling Place, this is My great longing. And it shall be, Stephen. But that is a work for yet another day.

"I want them to understand that I desire them as My friends, yes, even the whole of this people. That every heart would cherish Me and love Me, even as I have loved and cherished them. This is the thing that I have established in My heart. Because you have been faithful to that which I have called you, I will raise up to Myself one from your seed that shall lead them to Me. You will lead them into the Land. He shall lead them into the Promise. It is not possible that these today will enter into their new lands and find Me as their All, for the heart of this people is faint and cannot endure great change. I will make them strong and bring them to the place where they are able to receive and honor Me in all things. I will forgive their small courage and heal them so that they are able to stand before Me as a people holy unto My name.

Go and strengthen them with My words. I am always with you, do not be afraid. All the land is before you, Stephen, Strong of Heart. Be to My people a leader who shows forth My praise in the earth."

Stephen stood after a long moment, allowing the sweet aroma that filled his soul to have its perfect work. He looked about him beholding the beauty of the grove and realized that it was but a poor reflection of all that was within the heart of Him with whom he had communed through the night.

The words he had been given were still echoing in his mind when Shayla's gentle touch brought him fully back to the world around him. He heard the lifting laughter of youth and saw the two once-orphaned children running into the grove as he turned to look into the dazzling green eyes of his wife. In her face he saw love unfeigned. Evidence of their mutual love, in her arms she held their son, Shayle, who himself held tightly to a lock of her rich brown hair that had fallen into his reach. Stephen was amazed at the child's strength. "Not more than a score of days old and already has he the grip of a bear!" He took the child in his hands, loosing his hold on the lock of hair and lifted him into the air. "You are to be great in the sight of the Father of Spirits, Little Bear. You are destined to be His own and so shall you be. None shall stand before you and all that rise against you shall be put down."

Shayla grimaced at Stephen's foretelling and he noticed this. "Are you afraid for our son, my love? I tell you the truth, none have to this day been so favored in the sight of Him who called us. The angels of heaven shall bare him up and shall allow no harm to befall him. While he may be **hurt**, he shall never be **harmed**. I tell you, he is blessed by the Sure Hand!" His laughter sounded as a shower of refreshing cool rain upon a parched and barren ground as he spun around with Shayle held high in the air. She could not resist his joy and found herself entwined in his arms. The two children clasped to their legs at the sight of their laughing and hugging one another and thought to make a game of it. The five of them formed a circle of laughter as they danced together in the celebration of life.

They had used the days well since the speaking forth of the foretelling at Shayle's birth. The cool evening winds were giving way to warm nights and preparation was under way for the clan to cross the Triall. The waters were most shallow at the sandy beach where the washing was done. A rope formed from a weaving of strong vines would be used to ferry their goods across. Two barges of strong young saplings were constructed. Skins of otter were sewn in such a way as to trap air inside them and then they were sealed. These were lodged under the barges to keep them riding high in the water. Using long poles, the barges were easily moved along the path directed by the rope. In this way, the clan could cross over the river without so much as wetting a boot.

Because the people knew their wanderings in the Wilderness of Cann were over, the dwellings were all dismantled and their materials bundled and tied together. Each family gathered with their belongings beside them and waited until it would be their time to cross. Three men were to bind themselves with the rope and swim across the river. After securing the rope they would signal for the first barge to cross. They would receive and unload it. Once the barge was unloaded, two men would then take the barge back across, while the second loaded barge was being ferried.

Although the currents were strong and the water cold, the three who now strained against the pull of the vine trailing behind them in the water had been well chosen. As the first of the three clansmen climbed up the far bank of the river, he fell face down upon the ground, not in exhaustion, but in worship of the Father of Spirits. He was soon joined by the other two clansmen and the three of them lifted their voices in praise. After a time of holy thanks, they rose to their task. The rope was quickly secured and the steady rhythm of work set in.

In this way, the entire clan was transported over the Triall in half a days time. By late afternoon the vine had been cut, the otter skins retrieved and the barges given to the river.

The people were not too tired to express their elation of finally coming home! I tell you, they fairly rioted with joy! The singing and dancing that evening was such as to inspire the songs of countless generations of celebration. The fires were banked high and roasted meat was kept turning late into the night. Fresh cool honey mead flowed freely and none knew sadness. Sorrow truly seemed to be a thing so far away that one's mind could not remember the days of grief, so great was the gladness and joy of the new day. May it be forever so!

The following morning (not too early, for Stephen had mercy on his people) after all had broken fast and the animals were tended, Stephen urged his people into the lands of Ability. Dunn and Aieda were given places of honor at the head of the clamorous procession. Shayla tended the orphans and seemingly half or better of the clan's children, as befitted her calling. Cutter followed as protector of the honored, with the rest of the clan taking up places in accordance with their friendships and clan associations. Scouts ranged far to the front and both flanks. The multitude stretched out as far as the eye could behold.

And at the back, trailing at the very last, was one vigilant faithful servant, cradling his young son in his arms... a son who would one day lead this people. But first he must learn to follow. Stephen, through the dust raised by many feet, whispered words of comfort and joy to his son, whose tiny smile offered all the companionship he needed.

About the Author

Gary Zackery spends most of his days looking for an extra hour he can manipulate into another project or errand! His days are filled with work and play and a day ends when there is no more energy or resources to pull from.

Gary rides a Harley and frequently takes it to the prison where he and his wife, Diann, minister weekly. Gary and Diann like to fish, but seldom find the time to do so, even while living on a private lake. (The water is literally fifty feet from their back door.) His parents live in the North Texas area, as well as seven siblings.

Gary and Diann are Christians first, and they are entrepreneurs. Diann owns and operates a supply business. Gary is a small business consultant and executive coach as well as a Faith Based Anger Management Specialist.

They are intrinsically immersed in House Church. They ride motorcycles together with the Christians they meet with in home meetings as well as with the Christian Motorcyclists Association (CMA). They are both involved regularly in prison ministry. Gary is also a Gideon. They're hobbies include drag racing, fishing, and the rare occasion of being home to piddle around the house. You can learn more about Gary's business activities by visiting him on the web at www.StartRight.us. You may contact him by email at Gary@StartRight.us or by phone: (936) 291-2711.

If you enjoyed Stephen, I'd like to Recommend for Your Reading Pleasure:

I LOVE YOU MOM
PLEASE DON'T BREAK MY HEART

What the media is saying about
"I Love You Mom, Please Don't Break
My Heart" by John Borgstedt

* * * * *

"John Borgstedt holds nothing back in this true story of faith and change. It's one of the most powerful stories of survival ever told." Cindy Aguirre-Herrera -- Seguin Daily News

* * * * *

As a work of fiction, "I love you Mom, please don't break my heart" would be the kind of novel that leaves you up a little longer at night wondering what would happen if the story were true. Knowing that John Borgstedt's story isn't fiction, however, breaks your heart for John and all those who suffer through such circumstances. Thank God, literally, for John's ability to tell this story with such honesty and poignancy so that others may not turn a blind eye to such horrors. But this isn't a story of horror; it's one of hope! "Jayson Larson - Athens Daily Review"

* * * * *

"In I love you mom: Please don't break my heart, John Borgstedt tells of his young life and the abuse he suffered at the hand of his mother. It is a difficult to read tale, but the story does not end there. He is a survivor who visualized a better future for himself in public speaking forums at prisons, boys camps, and even in the courtroom as an advocate for child safety." Janice Ernest, Editor "WhileUWait" magazine

* * * * *

CPSIA information can be obtained at www.ICGtesting.com
Printed in the USA
LVOW040652101212

310878LV00002B/404/P

9 781456 727116